Our Father Who
Art in a Tree

Random House New York

Our Father Who
Art in a Tree

A Novel

Judy Pascoe

Originally published in Great Britain by Viking, a division of Penguin
UK, in 2002.

Library of Congress Cataloging-in-Publication Data
Pascoe, Judy.
Our father who art in a tree : a novel / Judy Pascoe.—1st ed.
    p. cm.
ISBN 0-375-50799-X (alk. paper)
1. Fathers and daughters—Fiction. 2. Paternal deprivation—Fiction.
3. Fatherless families—Fiction. 4. Fathers—Death—Fiction. 5. Grief—
Fiction. 6. Girls—Fiction. I. Title.
PR9619.4.P37 O97 2003
823'.92—dc21   2002021317

Printed in the United States of America on acid-free paper
Random House website address: www.randomhouse.com
98765432
First U.S. Edition
Book design by Mercedes Everett

For Noel Edward Pascoe

Our Father Who
Art in a Tree

It was simple for me, the saints were in heaven and guardian angels had extendable wings like Batman and my dad had died and gone to live in the tree in the backyard.

Weeks he'd been calling out, imitating the way I called over the back fence to my friend Megan. I didn't get the joke though; there was my dead father trying to get my attention and talk to me in a way I might understand, and every evening was the same. I thundered up the garden past the tree and sped up the back stairs, humming a mad tune all the way, trying to block out his voice.

The first time I heard him call was the evening after we'd been to the cemetery. I'd stood at his grave and watched the ants crawling across the dry earth; their pinhole nests perforated the red soil. It was too scary, I'd said to myself, meaning the ants.

"Don't worry about the ants." That's what I heard him say.

I replied in my own mind. "They're everywhere, why are there so many?" Meaning, "Is that you I'm talking to?"

"They're busy," he'd said. "Yes, it's me."

I hated thinking of him underground. I'd dreamt one night he pulled a rope and a light turned on in his dark coffin. The dream was a cross section of earth. There was a thin green line of grass, then a weight of brown earth, then my father lying in the coffin, with a bare bulb by his head illuminating the box.

That afternoon I stood at the back fence. Between me and the house was the great tree, enormous and dark with hanging branches dipping so low they brushed the carpet of coarse couch grass. It loomed above me, looking down on me like a giant. A circle of leaves at the top of the tree moved.

I bolted across the grass on my pin-thin legs, holding my breath and running like billy-o past the tree. I could hear it calling to me in much the same way I called to Megan when I lamented by the dry paling fence.

"Me-gan," I would call, dragging the word out for up to fifteen seconds. It drove the neighbors mad. Mrs. Johnson, who lived on the other side of the tree, protested to my mother.

"Does she have to call out like that? Sounds like a wounded animal."

"Me-gan," I called the second time. Starting with "Me-," then sliding down a note to "-gan," dragging out the *n*, annoying the suburb with my migrating goose call.

The tree calls, "Simone," with the emphasis on the

"-on." The second time it calls, it extends the "-on," as I do with Megan's "-gan," much longer than I think it needs to; trying to get my attention. The third, more desperate plea always comes as I reach the back stairs, and it lasts all the way up the twenty-two steps until I have slammed the back door too hard.

I flop down at the kitchen table. My mother's back presents itself as her front, married as it is to the electric frying pan. Although, in the last three months she has barely cooked and it's been my brother's back I've become more familiar with. Her pores widen in the heat from the sizzling meat.

Three festering grins in various states of disinterest watch as I sit at the kitchen table. Christ hanging from what appears to be like a great plus sign looks down on me, the eternal victim, and the orange seersucker tablecloth mixes with the fluorescence of the bar light above to color my tanned skin tobacco yellow.

Much later, after fifty spelling words revised half-heartedly at the kitchen table in the pools of dampness left after it had been wiped clean in random circles by Edward, my eldest brother, I put myself to bed.

"Simone. Simone." I thought I heard the tree, its voice whispering through the screens.

I eventually flung back my covers and dashed across the floor to my brother's bed, ramming an elbow into his side and pushing him in his sleep closer to the wall to make room for me.

The tree was quiet for some minutes and I lay watching the space in my empty bed where I should have been sleeping.

Through the stud walls I heard voices conferring; gentle murmurings and the reassurance of Mr. Reardon. His chocolate brown eyes unblinking as he watched my mother weep. The dark timbre of his voice rose from a baseline of shuffling papers.

I had seen my mother standing on the kitchen chair after dinner while Edward was mopping the table in idle circles and James was wiping the dinner plates. I looked up from my spelling to see my mother's calf muscles flexed as she stood on the chair and stretched to reach the shelf on the top of the hall cupboard. Mr. Reardon was the accountant for the church, and now he shuffled the papers that lived in the shoe box from Edward's size fourteen and a half black school shoes. I heard the rise and fall of their voices. My mother sobbing, Mr. Reardon consoling, then more shuffling of papers. The scratching of a pen on paper, then the voices moving to the front door. The closing of the heavy glass door. Then the light feet of my mother, the dragging of a kitchen chair across the tiles, and the shoe box being lifted back into place.

Gerard sniffled in his sleep, and his arm thrashed out. I was thrust out of bed as he rolled over to take up the space he had previously occupied. He had no idea, I thought as I crawled across the floor to my bed, sleeping with his teddy, waiting for school to start; he'd find out then you couldn't spend all day playing.

Outside the tree frogs belched and I made a dash for my bed, jumping the last bit. I pulled the covers up and put a pillow over my head and attempted to sleep, but my mother's tears were too loud to ignore. I tried to block them out. "Hello, Catholic sitting on a log." I repeated the stupid phrase I had heard the children from the state school call at me. They hid behind the grasshopper-infested hibiscus tree growing out of a black tire on Mr. Beatty's footpath and tortured me with the meaningless phrase that I now sang over and over to try to banish the sound of my mother's tears and my father's voice from the tree outside, which had quietened now to a wheezing breath.

I pushed the door to my mother's room open. I felt the weight of her pain in the walls and in the cupboards. The furniture was full of it. There was heat from her tears. My mother jumped when she saw me, then she opened her arms.

"I'm sorry, love, I'm crying again."

"I know," I said, crawling into the hug.

"I'll stop. I'm sorry."

It wasn't the right time to tell her that Dad was in the tree outside. When would I find the correct moment to let her know that she could go and talk to him if she wanted to.

Chapter 2

"Megan," came a call from the laundry door. *"Come in now."*
The voice waited for dissent but received none.

"Coming," Megan called back to her mother and
jumped down from the huge carriage-like swing we were
sitting on. It tipped back unexpectedly, giving me an eye-
ful of upside-down sky. There was a scalloped edge of orange cloud in the west, pinpointed with a bright white
light.

"Evening star! Saw it first," I said, landing beside
Megan.

"You win," she said, skipping down the cement path
that led to her laundry door.

Over the fence at the Lucases' house the light above
the stairs switched on, and Mr. Lucas swung out of his
back door. He strolled down the steps, stopped for a moment to consider the evening light, then turned on the

garden hose. Lying across the backyard, it wriggled like a cut snake as the water lurched through it.

I opened the gate on the paling fence that separated my garden from Megan's. The blackened wood was spattered with curly green fungus, bleached to white by the summer sun.

The gate swung shut and the lock dropped as the purple dusk fell.

"See you tomorrow," I called, but Megan had already disappeared into the dark antechamber at the back of her house.

"I've got spelling." I spoke to no one in particular, then I turned to face the tunnel of darkness before me.

"Simone," I could hear my mother. The screen on the back door softened her voice and gave it a lilac tone.

"Coming," I replied.

The melody of our voices was like a lilt crisscrossing the suburb.

I prepared to run across the grass. This afternoon, though, the tree was silent; it had stopped its mournful calling. So then I knew my dad was dead, the ants had got him now, well and truly. I didn't bother to run up the yard. I walked slowly, getting used to the fact that he was no longer in the tree; maybe he never had been.

The next thing I knew I was climbing the wood ladder nailed to the base of the tree, just to make sure he really had gone. I climbed higher, there was no sign of him, still higher I went, checking for his occupancy, until I found myself perched on a branch at the top of the tree, peering out at a dusk whisked with great spraying fans of cloud.

I'd climbed the tree a hundred times, but never beyond the fuzz of foliage, now below me, to this new throne, this new perch I had found ten feet farther on. That last stretch had made all the difference. The extra blanket of silence that layer of tree provided blocked out the noise of the world, muffled it, so there was only the last tuft of green above me, then the sky. Now there were other sounds, other voices, and a wind through the branches in a different pitch, the beating of birds' wings, and a voice coming from over my right shoulder.

"It's taken me a while to realize where I am" was how he started. "I woke up and saw your grandfather, and then I realized I was dead."

It was my dad talking. I think I nodded because it was so exciting to discover what I'd always known. If you climbed high enough in the tree in our backyard you came to another world.

"I realized then that I'd left you all. I didn't mean to die," he said. "But it's not that bad. Tell your mother I'm all right. I'll always love her."

The world suddenly seemed perfect from where I sat. Cupped in the fork of the tree, I felt as if my father were holding me. I remembered him again, not as a dead man buried in anty soil but as a living person. The wind filling his old gardening shirt, making it billow out from the ash gray hair on his chest. This was a father I had already forgotten, the father who went to work and came home, who sat in the now empty chair at the end of the table, who could swim and do math, whose wallet was always open. I didn't hate him now so much for dying, because for the first time since he died I could remember what he was like when he was alive.

The clouds on the horizon had settled into a dots-and-dashes pattern that encircled the suburb. I was starting to feel cold. It was winter now, and the mornings were so icy that I kept my clothes at the end of the bed so I could get dressed under the covers when I woke up. The sun didn't carve a path across the sky with the same intensity as it would in a few months. Then the heat that could melt the bitumen and fry your face to bright red would return, and the grown-ups would be complaining about that; right now they were irritable about the cold.

Then below, the sounds of the mortal world seeped in. Megan's father and her brothers had finished tea and were in their garage. They were lowering the model railway set with ropes and pulleys from the side wall of the corrugated garage. I could hear the transformer vibrating on the chipboard table as the train began whirring around the track, revving up the hill to a station where miniature people waited to board. In her kitchen Mrs. Johnson was clattering pans and emptying the contents of a saucepan through a sieve, the steam rising to fog her glasses. A line of bats flew almost silently overhead; then in the distance, a faint tinkling, milk bottle lids strung up to keep the crows away from Mrs. Pitteville's tomato plants.

All the sounds conspired to distract me from hearing what my father was saying. Then there was a scream from the back steps. It was my mother, her hand pushing a faceful of unkempt hair back from her forehead.

"Oh my God," she screamed, and her feet thundered down the boards of the back stairs. My three brothers followed behind her. Edward, my eldest brother, who was sixteen; then James, who I saw for the first time was taller than my mother, he was thirteen; then Gerard, the youngest, who was five. Their grins slipped slightly from their tracks when they saw how high I was in the tree. They looked frightened. I wasn't. Their voices were muted as they were funneled through the dew-beaded foliage. Louder in my ear was the voice of my father telling me to stay where I was.

The fire brigade came, but their truck couldn't fit down the side of the house. Hysterical now, my mother beat on the chest of the head fireman. I'd heard their sirens coming down the hill all the way from Keperra, past the drive-in movies, past the Redemptorist monastery where the old priests with ears the size of African elephants lived, past the playing field shaped like a picture I'd seen of an amphitheater in Greece. I'd heard their sirens, but I didn't realize they were coming to rescue me. The fire crew had to deal with my mother, swearing at the tree, at my brothers. Screaming at them first to climb the tree, then to stop, then to climb, then to stop. Getting my age wrong when they asked her. Telling them I was nine, when I was ten and a quarter. Edward was below me somewhere. I heard him calling to me, not as my father had in two syllables but in one stern word—"Simone."

A ladder hooked onto the branch below. It was followed by a fireman's head.

"Hello, love," he said. He took my hand, and I started to back down the ladder. Easily I could have done it myself, I didn't need a fireman and a ladder to help me. I had an audience below. Little figures like the people waiting on the platform of Mr. King's train set, they stood in their backyards looking up. I waved down. Megan was below on her carriage-shaped swing straddling the seats like a Russian acrobat, rocking the swing back and forth and waving.

"I can get down myself," I said.

"Yeah, well, I'm here now," he said, "and your mother's having kittens down there. So let's use the ladder."

Chapter 3

I was punished. Put in my room and told to stay there until I was sorry and had thought about what I'd done. Which I did, and the more I thought about it, the more I wanted to climb the tree again. So I wouldn't say I was sorry. I finally admitted guilt because I was hungry and ended up with a peanut butter sandwich in my room at nine o'clock. Edward smirked when I emerged from my room. He was studying in an alcove by the back door where the sewing machine lived.

"Good one," he said.

"Yeah right." I ran into the kitchen and straight to the fridge.

He lifted his chemistry book, a huge volume as thick as a shoe box. Of a similar weight were his physics and biology books. The three together were so heavy I could barely lift them when they were packed in his case for school. Behind the great tome were a stash of biscuits and a glass of red drink. He gave me a sip and a handful of biscuits.

I ate them in my room, with the peanut butter sandwich, hoping my little brother Gerard, who had only just fallen asleep, wouldn't wake up and start whining. When my mother came to retrieve the plate, she knelt by my bed like a repentant sinner and prayed. "God, I thought you were going to die," she started. "I couldn't have lived beyond that."

Then her tone changed. "But if you ever do that again, I'll thump you, so help me God."

Amen, I thought. It was a type of prayer.

Then she left, taking the plate and the crusty remnants of my stale sandwich. I was still hungry, so I waited a few minutes before I crept out again. The fire brigade had gone now and been replaced by Mr. Lombardelli. He had come to speak with my mother. Most of the Misters, as we called them, came to talk to my mother about money and wills and investments and taxation, but Mr. Lombardelli, an Italian migrant who lived in the next street, had come to give my mother a recipe book and some hints on feeding three boys.

"Pasta." He kept singing its praises. "You can eat it with steak, and here's a mushroom sauce. My mother's recipe." I heard him as I crept past and up the hall to my brother who still sat studying in the sewing alcove. Unwillingly he divided the remainder of the biscuits.

"Death," I could hear Mr. Lombardelli by the front

door—it hadn't taken long to move from food to death. "Is never fair," he continued. "My father died when he was fifty, and my grandfather is still alive. Where's the sense in that!"

"No sense," my mother said and closed the front door. I ducked into my bedroom before she could see me. I had only just crawled under the sheet when she came in. She knelt beside my bed, placing Mr. Lombardelli's heavy recipe book beside me, and she dropped her head onto my pillow.

"What's heaven like?" I said.

"How should I know?" she answered.

"Katherine Padley said you live in wonderful houses and you can watch television all day."

"That sounds all right then," she said, picking up the recipe book and moving toward the door. Across the hall in a block of darkness, James was already asleep; Gerard, in the bed opposite, was snoring like an old man.

Then something made me say it, though I felt embarrassment and a beating in my heart.

"Dad said to tell you he's all right," I mumbled.

She was already in the hallway, but enough of what I'd said had reached her.

"What did you say?" She turned on the heels of her bare feet.

"I didn't say anything."

I felt so scared. Too terrified to give her the rest of the message from the top of the tree. She rushed at me.

"Don't joke about things like that." She was in my face now, the Italian cookery book squeezing the breath out of me.

My mother was a wild nimble woman, tiny and out-grown now by two of her children. Her eyes were streaked with brown, imperfect blue, and as she leaned over me, I smelled her stale hair; she hadn't bothered to wash it for weeks. I felt ashamed for her.

"I'm not joking," I said.

As she walked back to the door, I felt impelled to speak. "Dad . . . ," I started.

She turned.

"Dad said . . ."

She moved back toward me. The air was puffing from her nostrils, in and out. I could see it.

"Dad says he'll always love you."

"Don't do this to me," she breathed in my face.

"I spoke to him. He's in the tree," I said.

For a long time she didn't speak. Then without a word she walked out of the room, closing the door behind her. The light from the hall narrowed to an L-shaped slit, and I felt as bad as I'd ever felt. She never closed doors, but I was too frightened to get up to open it.

Chapter 4

It must have been hours later when Mum shook me awake. I knew it was late because the house creaked in a way it only ever did in the lonely hours after she went to bed. I noticed she wasn't in her pajamas, she was dressed. The shadow from the branches of the tree dipped and swayed on the wall above Gerard's bed.

"Come on." She pulled my covers back. "Show me."

I trailed down the back stairs behind her, taking care, as she had, to step over a loose board near the bottom. There before us, above us, around us was the umbrella of foliage of the tree.

"Am I going to climb up there?" my mother said. I ignored her question and led the way.

"You've done it before," I said.

"I've had four kids since then," she said.

She climbed up the ladder, then followed me up the

mast of the tree to the first branch. She sat for a moment, dangling her legs in the dark.

"This is all a dream, okay?" She locked eyes with me to make sure I was in agreement.

I nodded, and we resumed climbing. There were five branches that grew straight out from the trunk on the Kings' side of the tree. The distance between them increased the higher you climbed, but they could be scaled as easily as a ladder.

"How far?" she asked.

"All the way," I said. "Up there." I nodded to the top.

My mother screamed, "Oh my God," as a dark, triangular shape launched itself from the branch above into the night sky. It was only a fruit bat, but the stress of the climb was beginning to show. She leaned against the trunk, and I could see she was going to give in. I couldn't blame her; it made no sense to me now that we were climbing the tree in the back garden in the middle of the night. Even if I had spoken to my father there earlier that day. I was now beginning to doubt whether I hadn't made it all up. How did I know it was him? It could have been me answering my own questions.

I was desperate to be back in my bed listening to Gerard's snoring, but something made me go on. Maybe because it would have been so easy to turn back.

"This is far enough," Mum said.

"Come on." I led her up to the next part of the tree,

the forked branch that stretched almost to the weatherboarding of the house. I felt, as I had once or twice since
my father's death, that I was my mother's mother and she
was the child. I'd even forged her signature on a check to
pay for a school trip. It wasn't hard, there were no frills or
squiggles, just her name, Dawn O'Neill, written flat and
large like a schoolgirl's. I removed my headband and
passed it to my mother; she was struggling to see through
the wild curls of hair that kept falling across her face.

She wasn't a coper, my mother. She wasn't pretending
she was, or that she could carry on without my father. We
had been covering for her for weeks. Some days choosing
clothes for her to wear because she often went to leave the
house unaware that she was wearing one of Dad's jumpers
over the old slip she sometimes wore to bed. I had taken
over doing her hair, washing it in the sink when I could
convince her it needed it. While brushing it dry one day, I
noticed gray hairs that had come uncoiled from her curls;
they stuck straight up, and I prayed she would start to care
for herself before the gray took over and made her look
old. Most of the time, I liked that she wore her grief in her
tatty clothes and her feral hair. It reminded me every time
I saw her that our father had died, and I wanted to remember that every day for the rest of my life. I couldn't
imagine going a whole day without thinking of him.

"Go on." I knocked her arm with my elbow and motioned higher up the tree. "I'll wait here."

"What's wrong with here?" she asked.

"You have to go higher, otherwise you can't hear."

She climbed onto the next branch. I watched her spiral around the tree, surmounting the final branch before she disappeared into the arbor of dark foliage above me and, I assumed, made it up to the throne.

I don't know how long it was before the tinkling of my mother's laugh caught my ear. Her giggles drifted through the leaves and branches that separated us and made me smile. It was momentary, wiped away by their arguing, chased then by more silence, out of which rose my mother's voice.

"I don't care," she started. "Whatever the reason, you didn't have to go."

I waited to see what would happen next. The silence dragged on.

"You copped out. You left me. If you really loved me . . ." She was crying again. I slumped. This wasn't what I'd been hoping for. It wasn't why I'd dragged her to the top of the tree. I was hoping she would talk to Dad, be happy, and then start to laugh and cook and wash again.

"If you really loved me," I heard her, "you wouldn't have left me like this."

I searched above, trying to see her, but it was too dark, the branches were too dense. Then, unexpectedly, she laughed again. I breathed a sigh of relief, but no sooner had she finished laughing than the tears began.

I don't know how long we were up there in the tree, but when my mother emerged her face had been unburdened of some of its tension. She swung down the tree like an excited monkey. She hit the ground, crouched, and ran across the grass as if she was alighting from a helicopter, giggling or crying, I wasn't sure which.

"Good night." My mother waved to me when I reached my bedroom door, and for a moment I felt there was not even going to be a thank-you. She stepped lightly on as she continued down the hall. At her bedroom door she stopped, backed up a pace, and turned to me.

"There is a light," she said and squeezed my arm. "Now go to sleep."

I marveled at how, even after my leading her up the tree to talk to Dad, she could be so immersed in her own feelings, so insensitive to mine. She must have seen the disappointment in my eyes. "This is our discovery," she said.

"*My* discovery," I reminded her.

"So it is, love," she agreed. "But whatever you do, don't tell a soul."

Chapter 5

Through the window of the cubby house, I saw the tree shimmer its leaves. Megan and I were baking a pretend cake in an oven made from a cardboard box. We slid a bowl of hot water in it to bake the mixture of flour, water, and milk we had stirred together.

"Do you know what?" The movement of the tree prompted me to want to tell Megan about my dad.

"No, what?" asked Megan.

"I . . . um." Then I remembered the promise I'd made to my mother to keep the tree a secret. I so wanted to tell Megan. It only seemed right. We told each other everything.

I dived out through the cubby door with a saucepan. "I'm getting more water," I said as I sped down the cracked path to the laundry.

It wasn't fair not to tell Megan, but somehow I had to find the strength to swallow my secret. I didn't trust myself, so I trotted back up the path with the saucepan of hot water and said, "I've got so much spelling to learn," and I ran.

Megan was calling after me, but I kept running. I jumped through the fence, not stopping until I got to the top step, where I took one last look at the umbrella of tree that covered our house. Megan was still calling to me, but I didn't reply. I crashed into the kitchen to find the three boys at the table, their heads bowed.

"I had to tell them," my mother said.

I dropped into a chair, out of breath. I couldn't believe it. I'd just left my best friend in the most awkward way so as not to betray our secret, and my mother had blabbed, just like that.

She must have seen my fury. "I'm sorry," she said.

I sat beside Gerard, who seemed unaffected by the news. Edward had slumped into a silence similar to what had become James's normal state, and James was for the first time since the day at the graveyard crying.

"They had to know," my mother reiterated on her way to the sink. "He's their father too."

That night we were instructed to behave as normal, kiss our little brother good night, then when he had gone to sleep, we were to assemble at the back door and wait till dark, then take turns climbing the tree. But the boys had no desire to be involved in the venture. Edward sat in his alcove by the back door, occasionally looking up from his studying, and James, who also declined the suggestion of climbing the tree, preferred to stay sitting on the top step. I joined him there, and we waited for our mother, listening for sounds of her interchange with the night.

The evening wore on, and the rise and fall of the cicadas' buzz eventually died away, and in the interim before the tree frogs began, we slumped, bored with waiting but too nervous to go to bed without her. James leaned against the railing of the stairs, and I fell back against the weatherboards of the house. I picked at the flaking paint, wondering if she would ever return. I began to think she had gone to join our father when I heard a faint snuffling. I stood to see if I could find a better position to watch what was going on.

Edward was inside pouring himself another rum. The lock on the mirrored door of the drinks cabinet clicked shut. He scraped his chair back toward his desk and hid his rum and Coke behind his physics book.

It became obvious once the tree frogs' symphony had reached its crescendo and died away and the fruit bats had taken off from the mango tree by the back fence that our mother wasn't coming in. Edward packed away his books and we all went to bed, leaving the back door open.

Much later I heard her sneaking up the stairs. There were her footsteps heavy down the hall, not the same light gait as the evening before. There was a density in her step and the way she fell onto the bed, an emptiness, and something more terrible than all the nights I had heard her sobbing, a screaming silence. I stood in her doorway.

"This is worse, much worse." She rolled to face me. "I remember now what I've lost."

Her words jarred me, and they made me sad. I wondered when she would be able to be our mother again.

"I miss him more now than I did before," she said.

But it didn't stop her climbing the tree most nights and talking to him. Sometimes the commotion coming from the top of the tree was as noisy as a flock of bickering cockatoos. The tree would sway with their voices on those nights. Other times it felt frozen with restlessness, and occasionally, every so often, it would buzz with a joy. On those nights I was pleased for her, but resentful because her occupancy in the tree stopped me from visiting my father. I wanted to talk to him and could spend days locked in my own thoughts with him, but I felt my mother needed to visit him more than I did.

Chapter 6

"Oh God," I heard my mother say, and she called me to the toilet to show me four green frogs the color of limes cling-ing to the inside of the bowl.

"Look," she said, trying to flush them away. We watched the frogs swilling about in the current before they were sucked down the U-bend. The two of us kept guard to make sure they'd gone, but it wasn't long before they reappeared, crawling slowly back up from the bot-tom of the toilet.

Later that afternoon the toilet stopped flushing alto-gether, and an hour later, when Mum turned on the tap in the kitchen, a load of brown, gravelly muck poured out into the sink.

I'd noticed a snowballing of things falling apart around the house. Loosening boards, leaking fixtures, er-rant latches. A buildup of what I assumed were the jobs my father had done without us even being aware that he did them. They were just part of the constant stream of misdemeanors committed by a house against its occupants. Jamming drawers, cupboards falling from hinges. They all could have been and had been ignored, first because my mother had never dealt with them before, and second because they required a type of action she was incapable of—asking for help. Edward had done what he could, but planing down jamming doors and unblocking toilets were beyond him. It wasn't until we'd used the toilet in the Kings' shed for a couple of days because ours was blocked that my mother finally decided she had to do something.

I watched her struggle with the yellow pages. When she finally located a plumber's phone number and rang, he was on holiday. The message on his answering machine gave the number of an alternative plumber; she tried that, but no one was home.

"It's too difficult," she said, and Edward, who had been watching her perform for half an hour, prevaricating and mumbling into her mug of cold soup, was so frustrated he stood to leave the room. Then something drew our attention through the slats of the front blinds. It was a pair of legs running up the path of the Johnsons' house. The legs belonged to a plumber, and he was about to jump into his van and drive off.

"Quick. Stop him," my mother called.

Edward charged out of the house.

"Stop," she called over Edward's head, but Edward had already done that.

"Stop," she called again, though the man had stopped and was walking toward her.

I trotted up the front path behind my mother, nervous for her that she would be incapable of wording her simple request.

She pushed me aside. "We've got frogs in our loo," she said.

"And that's no good." The plumber's words joined onto the end of hers and seemed to make a perfect sentence.

He followed my mother down the side of the house to the septic tank. She pointed out the manhole cover, and we watched him lift it off.

"Same trouble as next door," he said, flinging the heavy square of cement onto the grass beside him. He peered inside, then he was gone, striding up the side of the house toward his van, stopping for a moment to stare up at the tree on the way.

"Great tree," he said. "No good for your drains though."

A minute later he came back down the hill carrying some drain-clearing device. He fed the arm of it down into the dark pit of the septic tank, glancing once at my mother. In that instant he took in the mess of hair, the odd unmatching clothes, the bare feet, and the uncertain eyes. He seemed to see it all and know it.

"Stand back," he said as a load of chopped roots and mashed cockroaches spewed across the grass in front of us.

They stood together for an hour hosing the chopped roots down the yard toward the back fence. The spray from the hose plumed above them as they continued to talk into the orange dusk.

Edward had got fed up waiting for her and was cooking burgers in the electric frying pan. He squeezed blobs of tomato sauce over each lump of meat, then flipped the round of meat onto a bed of tomato sauce. We sat around the kitchen table eating and trying not to feel like we were waiting for our mother. Only Gerard objected openly by kicking his legs hard against the wall behind him. Finally Edward pushed him to the back door. I watched him from the top step run down the yard to our mother. She picked him up, and he stuck to her, his legs and arms clinging like the legs of the frogs hanging on the porcelain toilet bowl.

When she finally came inside, even under the flat fluorescence of the kitchen light, I could see that her face had gained an evenness. The corners of wildness that had moved in months earlier seemed to have leached away. She took Gerard to the bathroom, washed his face, cleaned his teeth, and tucked him in his bed. Then she came into the kitchen to tidy up. The counter was a row of bowls and plates covered in a film of flour from Edward's cooking. She wiped away the powder, then started scratching at the burnt meat on the frying pan. Then she found her washing up gloves and began to clean.

The noises of the house were different that night. Scrubbing and scouring, mopping and brushing. Buckets were filled, and tidal waves of grubby water were emptied. She dusted the top of the kitchen cupboards, she pounded rugs, poured disinfectant into her sponge, and wiped everything—the doors, the handles, the windowsills, under the kitchen table. Then the clearing began. The acres of sympathy cards and letters from distant relatives focusing on a memory or a phrase about our father—they had been scattered across the dining room table—she piled them up and put them in a box.

I lay in bed and listened to the rubbing and scratching, then the purposeful steps of my mother transplanting her tidying frenzy into another part of the house—her room. Cupboard doors creaked open, and I heard the *flumph* of clothes being tossed onto the floor. The sound became lighter as the pyramid of possessions grew. Then a rattling in the very top cupboard, papers and boxes being lifted out. I stood by my door and listened, concern pressed into my brow. Did my dad know his stuff was being evicted from the house?

The back door rattled, and I jumped. My mother, who was careening around her room with boxes and colliding with the cupboard doors, stopped. We waited. Me, my mother, my brothers, the tree, all waited for the second knock. It was the drain man, we all knew that, with his smile and a bottle of beer.

I peeked around the edge of my curtain. I could see him on the top step. My mother had slunk to the back door, I saw her caught behind the screen. She hesitated, then I heard him say her name.

"Dawn."

My mother was twitching and jigging and sidestepping.

"Come in. No," she said, staying safe behind the screen door. "Go," she said. "Come in. No, go."

I wondered, as did the drain man, what she meant. I noticed her eyes darting in the direction of the tree.

"I'm sorry. Tomorrow? I know I said tonight, but . . ."

"Dawn, I'll leave this here." He raised the bottle of cold beer he had in his hand. "Tomorrow night, maybe," he said, and then the drain man left, his feet turned out in his workmen's boots as he hopped down the back stairs, the cold bottle of beer left on the top step.

The door opened, and my mother skimmed down the steps, taking the bottle of beer on the way.

That night the tree shook with jollity. It was a forced laughter though, I assumed a result of my mother's guilt.

While my mother was visiting my father, I crept into her room and found his possessions piled on the bed. Boxes of papers stacked by the door for disposal. The curtains were drawn so he couldn't see in, as if she was trying to hide the fact that he was being moved on. When she returned later that night, barefoot and merry from the beer she had drunk in the tree, she replaced the pile of clothes. I heard her rehang each shirt and refold each jacket and pair of pajamas. The heat I had felt from the tree when the drain man was on the back steps abated, and the animals went about their business, trawling the sky and organizing the food for the next day.

Chapter 7

My mother saw the gray heads of the women first, bobbing up and down through the venetian blinds, like a line of yachts seesawing toward a finish line.

"What are they doing?" Mum said, watching the women. Like a determined flank of soldier ants they marched closer to our front door.

"What do they want?" She jogged nervously on the spot.

The inevitable knock on the door sent my mother into a spin, zigzagging across the cool wooden floorboards. We dived for cover. The sight of the women on our front porch struck the same chord of recognition in all of us. They resembled so completely the gray stream of women who came to our house the afternoon after our father's funeral. It brought back the pots of tea, the muffled voices, the sniffling, the occasional howl, then the sound of tissues being plucked.

It was a terrible return to that fearful hot day. The heat in the church had been unbearable, even with all the doors open. That much black cloth on a hot day with only the ceiling fans to churn up the air can push the temperature beyond the tolerable.

It was too much for the old folk. Aunt Kit folded at the knees ten minutes in, and the rest of the church swiveled to watch as she drifted to the pew, so convinced were they that she was going to drop dead and upstage the service and the untimely death of her niece's husband. Waiting for such an event, Uncle Jack in the seat behind extracted the smelling salts from his chest pocket. Once Aunt Kit had come round and her hat, a flat, black saucer darted with a purple feather, was rearranged on her white tufts of hair, Uncle Val offered her his hip flask of brandy. When it became clear Aunt Kit was revivable and she'd had more than a few nips of brandy, the congregation returned to their ruminations. They bowed their heads to the power of their Creator, they thanked him again that it hadn't been their turn this time.

I could see from my seat beside my mother, through the wall of louvered glass, my class lined up outside the church. The blood red glass was difficult to see through, but the yellow and orange panes were less opaque, though they distorted the faces, giving all my classmates monstrous chins and shallow foreheads.

The heavy box in the aisle beside us seemed too black

for my father. I wished it was decorated, painted with some swirls and messages.

Now, as the women we associated with that day, the busy beavers who had supplied the tea and sandwiches at our house for the mourners—as they came down our path we scattered in fear, leaving our mother to open the door.

"Yes?" Her bare feet and thin legs greeted the women. Gladys Havelock led the way, holding up her Neighborhood Watch folder. "Dawn, it's your turn."

Mrs. Sanders patted my mother on the arm on her way into the house. "I thought you were going to remind her," she whispered to Gladys.

"Didn't I?" Gladys looked at my mother, who shook her head.

"Too late, the gang's all here." Gladys clamped the clipboard to her side.

The mass of gray-haired widows pushed into the lounge, pressing elbows into each other's sides and exchanging worried glances. The unspoken consensus seemed to be it would be good for everyone to continue to act normal.

My mother watched the stream of women take up their seats in her front room. They shuffled and sighed and waited to be offered tea. But Mother didn't drink tea; so she didn't offer.

"Anyone have anything to report?" Gladys started.

"It's been dark, this last week, at night," said Mrs. Sanders.

"I've seen someone dark," Mrs. Drummond, old and deaf, chipped in.

"Were they black?" Mrs. Layton was on the edge of her seat trying to choke back her fear.

"Very." Mrs. Drummond hesitated. "Black as the night. I couldn't really see they were so black."

"I saw *you* looking at something the other night," said Mrs. Sanders.

"I was watching Sandra." She nodded toward Mrs. Layton.

"I was watching Daisy." Mrs. Drummond referred to the woman sitting next to her.

"I was watching Gladys." The old woman spoke gruffly, not sure what she was being accused of.

"What were you watching, Gladys?" Mrs. Layton sucked in her lips, and the skin of her chin shriveled.

"I thought I saw you, Dawn." Gladys leaned over to my mother. "Up your tree."

Lying on the cold tiles in the hall, I slid an inch closer to see how my mother would respond. There was a pause, and it felt to me like the ceiling was starting to lower. They'd seen my mother up the tree. They might try to take her away from us, that was my first thought.

I noticed though she didn't comment. I saw her perfect nonreaction. Mrs. Layton tried again. "There has been a lot of noise coming from up there, the last week."

"Maybe it was the fruit bats." My mother spoke without a hint of sarcasm.

Her face had tensed slightly, but no more than it was already from being confronted in her own home by a group of uninvited pensioners.

It was true my mother had made very little effort to cover her tracks. The Johnsons, who lived directly beside us, were old, and the Kings behind had a noisy house full of children, so she was safe from the nearest neighbors. But she had made no attempt to conceal her tree climbs or to disguise the noise they made. Especially the night the drain man called; after he left she was so loud I was sure the entire suburb must have heard. Vonnie, who lived next to Megan's house and directly behind the Johnsons, saw my mother struggling for another excuse. She cut in.

"All the kids were up there again. I noticed the other evening." She sounded as if she was displeased, but there was a playful tone in her voice.

"After what happened, you'd think you'd be a little more careful." Gladys challenged my mother with a look of scorn.

"I see the roots have got in the drains again," she continued.

"Not badly," said my mother.

"Not what the Johnsons said." Gladys sounded very pleased with her private knowledge.

"It's been worse," Mum countered.

"Have you got any plans?" Gladys hadn't finished yet. "For the future, assuming present root growth continues.

Not that it affects our side of the road, but I would have thought your immediate neighbors may be interested."

"Doesn't bother me," said Vonnie. "And the Johnsons' backyard is so full of gum trees. It's questionable which tree is doing the most damage."

Mum was off the hook for the minute, thanks to Vonnie, and the old girls huffed and puffed and waited for the cups of tea my mother had no intention of offering them.

Chapter 8

Mother's trips to the tree stopped that night. Squashed like a jack-in-the-box waiting to have its lid lifted, she waited inside the house. I could hear her pacing in her room, and I knew she felt trapped there by the eyes of the old women of the suburb. I had continued to eavesdrop on the old women's conversation from the cold tile floor as they left the house that evening, clopping down the front steps with their bunioned hoofs stuffed into sandals.

"We all have dead husbands," I heard Gladys hiss into the ear of another of the old girls.

"She may have been a bit younger when she lost him, but so what?" another one said.

My mother heard them too, and she was furious. Then I saw her decide not to brew on it, and she broadened her thoughts. The next afternoon I discovered why. She must have thought that the only way to beat the enemy was to employ them. So during the cicadas' five o'clock chorus I was marched across the road with my first communion dress, which had sat for weeks in a paper bag crushed behind the door of my mother's bedroom. My mother called to warn Gladys that I was on my way over with the dress and a bag of beads that had been passed on from a cousin. She asked Gladys if as a favor she could alter the dress to fit me and do something with the beads, which had originally been intended to decorate the bodice, and since Gladys was such a wonderful embroiderer . . . I wondered, as she continued to flatter her, if Gladys was aware of the ploy. Which, I assumed, was that Gladys, by doing this favor for my mother, would be seen not only by God but also by most of the congregation to be helping a needy young widow. And if they didn't see it, they would hear about it, since her needlework was legendary. In the process of completing the task she would gain some empathy for the family and soften her attitude toward my mother and the tree. That was the plan, I think.

As I crossed the road the sun blazed down from above a row of unchanging suburban pines growing along Gladys's side fence. Her house was in the middle of the block of land, surrounded on all sides by grass burnt brown in the midsummer scorch. It was a perfect square, Gladys's house, and every window was closed—locked, barred, and bolted. The Neighborhood Watch sign on her front gate rattled as I closed the gate behind me.

Gladys opened her security door, and I felt the cold air from inside rush around my ankles. Unfortunately,

only the front room was air-conditioned, and standing in
Gladys's sewing room at the back of the house was like
being torched with a hair dryer. The stiff white fabric of
the dress prickled, and the chunky homegrown seam
where the bodice joined the skirt itched like mad. A line
of pins holding up the hem around the sleeve dug into me,
and the caramel carpet at my feet was like dirty sand clot-
ted with occasional brown boulders of old lady furniture.
It made me feel faint. I longed to escape. I looked around,
desperate to find a way out of the overtidied house full of
glass cases full of crystal and china.

"When's the big day?" Gladys asked me.

"Not until next year," I admitted, wondering if
Gladys would suddenly see through my mother's strategy.

I could see her wondering why my mother was so anx-
ious to have the dress done when my first communion
wasn't for another six months and Gladys knew my
mother wasn't the type to be overorganized.

"I can't promise anything," she finally said, picking
up the bag of beads. "I'm better with thread."

She tutted, then left the room.

"That's old, that dress," she called from the hall. I could
hear her digging around in a cupboard in the hallway.

"All my cousins made their communion in it," I answered.

She returned with a square of folded white silk, and I
knew immediately the material had been meant for her
own wedding. Gladys's fiancé, we'd all heard about him,

left to rot in the corner of a prisoner of war camp in Changi, Singapore.

She never married and she never got over it, that was how the story went, and once a year she met a thin man who had shared the cell with her fiancé. To pass the time in the camp they had bet on dice they made out of paper. He was so old now, the thin man, that he had stopped coming, and Gladys had to go and visit him in an old people's home.

The sheet of white silk landed on the Formica, and she started cutting, the scissors grating across the tabletop. She was going to make me a new communion dress from the fabric that should have been used for her own wedding dress. It gave me the creeps.

There was no way I was going to wear a dress made out of old lady material. I ran across the road to tell my mother. When I got there I was appalled to find her circling the base of the tree. Edward was in the kitchen trying to ignore her, the telltale film of flour covering the counters as he attempted to thicken the stew he was making with a cup of flour and water. James, Gerard, and I sat on the top step, watching her desperately tramping around the base of the tree like Pooh searching for the Heffalump. Eventually I couldn't stand it any longer, and I started down the stairs, imagining I would think up an excuse on the way to stop her and bring her inside.

"Dawn!" I heard someone say. The voice was deep and penetrated the wall of surging cicadas.

My mother froze. I stopped too, halfway down the garden, wondering where the voice had come from. For a moment I thought it was Dad, fed up with waiting for Mum to climb the tree to come and see him. Then I saw Vonnie at the bottom corner of the garden, leaning on a single gray fence post where the Kings', the Johnsons', and our backyards met.

"Leave him for a while, Dawn."

Mum was with Vonnie now by the back fence, and I was on the grass between her legs, my hands reaching up and grabbing at her calf muscles.

"You've got to let the dead get on with it," said Vonnie.

My mother was instantly accepting that Vonnie knew what was going on.

"I can't leave him alone," she said.

"Don't let him rule your life."

From the ground where I was lying, the tree appeared to have grown larger than our house.

"Go mad if I do," said Mum. "And mad if I don't."

Vonnie shook her head. I wasn't sure if she was agreeing or disagreeing. "You can't live with the dead," she finished.

"Can't live without them either." My mother's addendum.

Vonnie hauled a box of papaws onto the gray stump. "From the Lus." She flicked her head in the direction of the Vietnamese family who lived next to her.

"The fruit bats had a party last night." She pointed to a clump of papaw trees in the Lus' garden. In the failing light they resembled a row of women wearing great circular hats and carrying buckets on poles balanced across their shoulders. Mr. Lu's shovel rose and fell, and a pad of dirt hit the pile he had already scooped into his wheelbarrow. If I crawled through the hole in the Johnsons' fence, I could see the Buddha that sat under the macadamia nut tree on a plinth raised up on four bricks.

The tree blew up behind us, revealing the veined undersides of its branches. I felt as if it could grab me and lift me to the sky.

"I talk to Tom most days," Vonnie said, passing the papaws over the fence. "When I've got a minute, but not the other way round. I don't let him interrupt me. Unless it's important."

My mother nodded, keeping her back to the tree. A new resolve seemed to be spreading through her body; the arches of her feet rose to greet some new possibility.

"I've only lived for him these past few weeks," she admitted. "I've not cooked. I've not talked to them"—I knew she was referring to us—"I'm sorry, love." I lay my head against her thigh and allowed her to smooth my hair, pulling at bits and straightening them between her melancholy fingers.

"They understand that," said Vonnie. "But now give them some time. And be careful. Talking to the dead isn't something everyone understands."

"Vonnie, I'm grateful to you." My mother was crying. "I needed to be told, I'm sorry. I've lost it a bit these past few weeks."

With fresh determination we traipsed up the backyard and closed the door on the spreading arms of the poinciana tree, and Vonnie's clothes trolley rumbled back down her path.

Inside the kitchen Mum whipped the serving spoon from Edward's hand and hugged him. "I'm so sorry," she said, pushing him into a chair and serving the gluggy rice and burnt stew he had made. "It's going to be okay now. I'm back, I'm here again."

We watched her back as she stood at the kitchen counter serving the food, the back that was so familiar to us, that never lied. We wanted to believe what she said, because she was our mother and we needed to believe her, but something about her tone and the forced straightness in her spine made us fear the worst. She wanted to be with us, but she wasn't, not really.

Chapter 9

"My dad's up in the tree." I said it to Megan, just like that. Even though I'd sworn to Mum I wouldn't tell a soul, she had, and anyway, he was my discovery. So it seemed that I had the right to tell who I chose, and Megan was my best friend, and it just came out in a rush of words I couldn't hold back.

"I can see him," Megan said, meaning in the clouds we were watching. Her head was resting on the bar at the back of the swing, her feet were stretched across to my seat and mine to hers. She pointed to the sky. A fleece of clouds slipped past, riddled with holes. I searched through it for ages trying to find him.

"See his face?" she asked.

I couldn't. The cloud began to stretch. "He's gone now," she said.

"I don't mean he's in heaven. He's in the tree, I told you."

"Is he?" she asked.

I nodded. I could see Megan didn't believe me.

"Didn't he go in a box?" she said. Megan's sandy hair fell across her freckled face.

"Yeah he was, but now he's up in the tree."

"We don't go in boxes," said Megan. "We get burnt."

The swing rocked slowly, and her leg dipped down to the grass.

I couldn't work out which was worse, the silence of the box or the horror of the flames.

"I just want to be left," I said, "and I'll find my own way."

"They've got to put you in something."

"On the beach," I said. "If they have to. Wrapped in my favorite quilt."

Megan was looking again at the racing clouds above us. "Witch jumping over a hurdle," she said.

I watched as the witch's long white front leg grew longer and her face narrowed to a point.

"Now it's a dragon."

"I see it," said Megan.

"Becoming an angel."

"With a bugle."

"Over there." Megan pointed to a new bank of clouds. "Elephant with long toes."

The wind pulled at the cloud elephant, elongating its toes, bending them into talons.

"Claws," I said.

"Ribbons," Megan contradicted me.

"Claws," I said, louder, sitting upright and rocking our giant carriage-like swing. Megan dropped her head back to take another look, but our cloud elephant had already joined a froth of clouds on the edge of the sky.

"I want to see him then," said Megan, slipping down to the ground.

"You can't see him. You can only talk to him. Except we're all banned and Mum said they'd take her away if they found her up in the tree again."

"Take her away to where?" asked Megan.

"I dunno."

"You'd be like an orphan." Megan was excited.

"I might have to come to your school," I thought aloud.

"That'd be good."

I wasn't sure. "Do they do God at state school?"

"Course," she said.

"Can't be the same one as ours?"

We had to think about that. If we had the same God, then why did we go to different schools?

"It has to be different," I said.

We were baffled. "If I'm a special Catholic," I said, "at Catholic school—do they tell you that?"

Megan drew a blank expression. Obviously they didn't.

Was it all right we were different? Did it matter my school said it was better to be a Catholic and I was a better person because of it? They must be wrong, because I loved Megan and I wanted to spend every day with her forever, but I was still worried about her school. Who were all the children there? Would they hate me if I had to go there, because if they took Mother away, whoever they were, to this place, wherever it was, we might have to move and go to another school and be contaminated by children who weren't special Catholics. It was exciting and dreadful all at once.

"I'll meet you tonight," I said. "In the tree at the first branch. No sounds, though. If we get caught, Mrs. Johnson'll call the fire brigade again."

Chapter 10

The night was a throng of wildlife. Possums skidding across the roof and kicking mangoes to each other. Coiling their tails around branches and staring in the window at me with their glass eyes. Squadrons of bats patrolling the sky; tree frogs belching out their nightly chorus, and all underscored by the drone of the cicadas.

When things had calmed and the night was breathing again, I rolled to the door of my bedroom and stepped as quietly as I could down the hall. My mother was fidgeting in her room, but she rarely checked us again after she had done her nightly rounds.

Jesus and his throbbing heart watched me drop out of the house, scraping my stomach on the windowsill on the way down. As I fell, I cut my foot on a sharp branch of the rhododendron tree under the corner window. On the ground the grass stabbed at my feet, it was that dry in the western corner of the house. I wondered why I hadn't used the back door as I bent my leg up to try to see how bad the cut was. Surely the lock on the back door couldn't be as loud as my pained landing.

James and Edward were still awake, goading each other to sneak into the kitchen and steal food. What they ate amazed me, gargantuan meals followed by slice after slice of bread. James was putting on weight; his grief was silent and fed on bread and strawberry jam, the color of Our Lord's burning heart. Edward's grief was confused. He was torn between roles—husband, father, son? None seemed to fit. He tried to help Mum by talking to her after dinner about grown-up things, and Mum let him, but it was the string of Misters with whom she really relieved the burden of how she felt. Her grief was a monologue she could unload onto anyone. Somehow her broken dam of grief had blocked the rest of us. Ours was notched up in explosive arguments. Fighting over the remnants of a meringue pie a neighbor had baked or scuffles over seating arrangements.

Megan was waiting on the lowest branch. We'd climbed the tree many times before, so we scrambled up the first few branches easily. Taking turns then on top of the fifth to hug the tree, stretching a leg around the trunk until we could feel the dead branch on the other side. From the dead branch it was a step up to the snake tongue branch, so named because it divided in two as it traveled toward the house, its feathered end tickling the weatherboarding. This was the branch that rubbed against the house and threw a shadow across the wall above Gerard's bed.

Once on that branch, you had to shimmy up to the cave, a kind of hollow in the trunk with a fan of branches above. That was the place where I had first talked to him. If you waited for the bats and the possums to silence themselves, breathed three times deeply, then you could hear him speak. But as I waited on the snake branch, Megan straddling the tree to step on the dead branch heard a whisper coming from the veranda. She tapped my leg, alerting me to the low voices. I shrank to a ball on the branch and pulled Megan up.

Through the feathers of foliage we could see my mother's bare legs and the outline of the drain man leaning on the railing of the veranda. My mother was beckoning him to move along the veranda to the front of the house. As she disappeared into the shadow, I saw her throw a glance at the top of the tree. It was only a flash, a twitch on her forehead, but its minuteness spelled guilt.

We edged along the snake tongue branch until we could see them, the idea of communing with the dead quickly forgotten when there was real-life intrigue before us. We lay on either side of the snake's forked tongue and watched. We could just make out in the shadows that they were drinking a bottle of beer.

"That stuff's foul," said Megan.

"I know," I said. I could imagine smearing away the gooseflesh on the outside of the bottle with a fidgeting finger.

"Do they have sex?" Megan whispered across to my branch.

"No," I said. "He clears the pipes when the roots get in."

"Do we like him?"

"No," I said. "He likes my mother."

There was movement; their voices scooted around the edge of the house. My mother's mood had changed. She stepped back into the light. In and out of the shadows her face moved. The drain man was beside her. There was some demand from my mother, then a clipped reply from him. Then he was gone.

The tree began to vibrate. I could feel a rumbling. Megan looked spooked. "Let's get out of here," she said. We reversed down the tree quickly, the bark scratching at our bare legs.

We didn't speak until we reached the ground.

"I'll see you tomorrow," Megan said, anything but disappointed that she hadn't managed to speak with the dead. It was far more interesting for her to see my mother drinking beer in the dark with a plumber than it was to talk with my dead father.

"Yeah," I said, "I'll see you tomorrow."

Chapter 11

I'd only been back in my bed a minute when I heard a knocking on the wall behind me. I jumped with fright before realizing it was only the rats running inside the walls. Since Dad had died the rodents were worse. They knocked on the wall by the end of the bed, rapping on the timbers. I was too frightened to move. I was scared if I made a noise I wouldn't hear them chewing through the walls above my head. Then I'd miss the crucial moment to escape before they attacked me.

The volume of their scratching increased suddenly. It sounded like three of them were fighting, chasing each other in a whirlpool of rat limbs. I heard my mother stirring in her bed on the other side of the wall. She punched the wall hard with a book, trying to shut them up.

Then I heard the shattering of glass and my mother scream. I jumped from my bed and ran to her room and found her squashed against the bed head, her arms over her head. By her side, lying in her bed was the branch, the snake tongue branch. It stretched from the window across the room to the bed, where its feathered end lay draped beside her. When she dared to drop her hands from her face, I could see her expression change from fear to grief as she realized that the branch lay on my father's side of the bed.

That was when I first understood that whatever was between my mother and the drain man was serious, he wasn't just another Mister. I could see her recognize it as well, and now my father was letting her know he wasn't going to give her up that easily. Even if nothing was happening with the drain man, my father was aware that the intimate moments he had shared at the top of the tree with my mother were limited. Even though those moments seemed real, as real as any moment of dialogue any two living people could have, they could never share a bed again, their relationship could never involve the flesh. I understood then that there was something in the hardship of real life that was so vital it transcended the spiritual. The fact that Dad could never compete with the realness of human contact struck me like a blow. And there was this other thing called sex, and I didn't understand it or know what it was, but it had to do with beds and men and women and I realized I hated my mother for whatever it was she had done to make my father mad. There was this bed and two men involved, and I sensed that meant trouble. What I saw as Dad's attempt to assert his claim over my mother was so touching, I stood there, lost.

Edward arrived and gaped at the damage before him. My mother still hadn't moved. The bed and floor were covered in glass. She motioned for Edward to stay where he was, though his instinct was to rush over to her. She pointed to her shoes, thrown down in the corner of the room. Edward in bare feet leaned into the room and retrieved them. He threw them to her on the bed, and she slipped her feet into them and carefully swung her legs down to the floor. The fragments of glass scrunched underfoot, and she took her time getting to us. At the doorway she turned back to look into the room. It didn't appear as if she found it strange or out of place that the branch we called snake tongue, which had for years rubbed against the side of the house on windy nights, forcing me to lie awake listening to it grinding its bare knuckles on the weatherboarding, had flung itself into her room. My mother waved the damage away, shrugged it off as if it were an inevitable household accident waiting to happen. Like a top-heavy vase of flowers sitting in a gusty spot. She walked away from it down the hall, pushing Edward and me toward the bank of moonlight at the kitchen window.

It was near one o'clock, and somehow the excitement of having a reason to be awake in the middle of the night overtook us, and as my mother was oddly chatty we wanted to stay with her. Her moods were so unpredictable, any chance of being with her when she wasn't dark and erratic was to be cherished. There was a joy in her movement and her voice. Edward, I could tell, was appreciating it as much as I. She fed us, cooked a meal even with what felt like genuine love. It seemed a weird response to the drama. I put it down to adrenaline and the fact that her moods had become randomized after the shock of Dad's death. We were all in shock at the time, but we didn't know it. Whatever the reason for her cooking the meal, we were grateful, and just after two o'clock I went back to my bed feeling happy, until I remembered the branch.

I don't know where my mother slept that night, but I have a feeling it was in her bed amongst the devastation. That made me sad, because I thought she was going insane. I knew that meant we would have to keep looking after her, making sure no one knew about what was going on, and I cursed the day I climbed the tree and talked to my dad and believed that it would help my mother to tell her to climb the tree and talk to him.

The branch stayed where it was for the rest of the week, while my mother's moods continued to fluctuate. Mostly she seemed happy and in no hurry to have the branch removed from the side of the house and the damage repaired. It wasn't what most people associated with normal mother behavior. Mothers on the whole seemed to be cleaners by nature. Things that were broken were thrown out or fixed, drains had to be cleared, toilets unblocked, lightbulbs changed, saucepans scoured, that was natural mother behavior. Leaving a gaping hole in the side of your house with a branch sticking out of it was unthinkable mother conduct, irresponsible.

It was only when she found us using the branch as a tightrope that she was forced to act. As the week had gone on, we had begun to sneak into her room and dare each other to walk from the bed to the trunk of the tree. The rules didn't allow us to sit or use our hands in any way, other than stuck out from our sides, wavering, like those of a tightrope walker. It was much more dangerous than it looked. When you were standing on the bed, it was an easy enough dare, but once you were outside the window, the dense foliage shielded a view of the ground below, disguising the fact that it was a long way down.

Chapter 12

I didn't think then and I still don't that my father was the tree, or the tree, my father. The spirit of him or some memory or part of him was undeniably there, so it became the focus of our memory of him, past, present, future. It was how we kept him alive, forcing him to stay near us. How much of what happened with the tree was caused by his presence there is difficult to say, and skeptics find the suggestion of a connection ludicrous. What happened may have been coincidental, but it appeared as if the tree was acting like a jealous husband. It had lunged through my mother's window, grabbing for her, as if Dad were trying to make her join him in death.

It may have been that it was the gesture of a sad and lonely spirit wanting to do the most banal of human things, go to sleep in his own bed with his wife, a pleasure he had been robbed of. No matter which way I thought about it, seeing the branch on my mother's bed made me sad, but also terrified of the power of the dead.

The drain man turned up a few days later, saying he wanted to check our drains, he was still concerned about them. We knew it was really to see our mother. Seeing a living man and noting, though I was too young to put words to it, the way he looked at her, made me see the power of the living. It was immediate and grounded, not wafty and indefinite like our relationship with our father.

My mother and the drain man stood at either corner of her bed. The branch pinned across the covers wasn't a sight that was easy to comment on.

She had stalled him downstairs by the laundry for half an hour, trying to hide the damage in her bedroom above. It was difficult to see it from the ground, as the tree grew so close to the house. You could stand immediately below the catastrophe and be unaware of it. Eventually I noticed her maneuver him into a position where he could see the unbelievable sight of the branch skewering the house.

"Holy shit," he said. Then, "Sorry," when he saw we were all watching him.

Mother appeared to be reassured by his reaction somehow. He looked things over for a long time before he made any comment. "Jeez, Dawn. It's a bit freaky."

"Isn't it?" She finished his sentence using the same rhythm, in the weird way they'd had from the start.

The fact that she knew, that he knew she'd made no attempt to have the branch removed, magnified its strangeness.

"I guess I should do something about it," said Mum. "I just wasn't sure what to do. Where to start."

The drain man skirted the room, searching for a reason why my mother might be so odd as to want to keep the branch of a tree in her room.

He looked at her. "Are you serious?"

Mum just looked at him.

"I've heard about people building houses round trees. I wouldn't recommend it, though, the plumbing's a nightmare."

She smiled, and I saw her wonder for a second if she could let him in on her secret. Then I grasped the reason why she couldn't. They were standing by the bed; the air felt gluey with the tension between them. The weight of the heat seemed to allow them to look at each other for longer than I had seen grown-ups look at each other before—if that was what they were doing. His dark earthen eyes met her imperfect blue irises, and I knew that he was going to lie in my father's place, on my father's bed. I will never see my father again, I thought. He will leave us for good, if this man comes in here. This man who may have a wife, children. The children would have to come on weekends. I'd heard about this. I'd have to share my room with more boys, chances were he'd have three boys with names like Jack, Stephen, and Timothy, and then there would be six boys and me, and I held my breath until I fainted and toppled down onto the unvacuumed hall carpet. I came round a minute later and was sick over the gritty rug at the door of my mother's room.

I didn't have to worry about more children. My brothers and I discovered later that night when we listened to my mother and the drain man talking in a dark corner of the veranda that he did have children, two daughters, adopted from Malaysia, but they were older. He and his wife had fostered many other children but had no children of their own. This situation had placed a stress on their relationship that had eventually caused them to separate. We heard all this listening through the open window of Mother's bedroom. They were only feet away from us, but it was difficult to hear sometimes above the sound of the beating cicadas.

When we heard their chairs grating along the wood of the deck we scattered, but they were only topping up their glasses with beer. Finally the drain man left; we watched from the front window. Mum waved him off from the dewy grass of the footpath in her bare feet. I saw her sneak a quick look about her, checking to see if the neighbors were watching.

That night I heard my father calling to me again. I put a pillow over my head to stop the noise. I didn't want to talk to him. I went to my mother, but she wasn't in her room. Now that the branch had been removed, it seemed so empty in there. We'd become accustomed to it lying across the bed. The drain man had cleared it all away that afternoon. Lowering it with ropes like a coffin into a grave. The leaves had fluttered down in eerie circles.

"Simone," I heard my father calling me.

"No," I said, and I searched the house more desperately for my mother. I found her huddled on the sofa with the television on, watching a late movie. I saw her confusion as the black-and-white film flickered on her face. She didn't bother to take me back to bed.

For the next week she seemed to sleep anywhere but in her bed, and the tree began calling me again. It drove me mad, but she was cross with him, she said, for complicating her life, for leaving her, and for a while she turned her back on him. It seemed easier to think of him as dead than as partly living with us. His memory was an inconvenience, and though my mother didn't know it at the time, or maybe she did, it was stopping her getting on, stopping us all. It had been useful for her to be able to talk to him, but not so useful for living with the living. And the drain man was very much alive. He seemed to be life itself. The way he walked. He was cemented to the earth. It made my father seem even more dead. They were earth and air, and my mother was the fire between them. There was no water to be seen anywhere. Water may have lubricated it all, oiled the awkwardness that I felt between the three of them. The water that was there kept getting blocked in the drains.

Later that week I heard her scream. She was under the house. She was hanging the clothes there to dry because it looked like rain. I wasn't desperate to see what fresh horror she'd found, so I didn't hurry. I dawdled down the stairs and found her staring at a tree root that had churned a path across the cement in its search for water. The knuckles of the root protruded like the joints of an arthritic hand that was attempting to straighten. We could see that one of the wooden stumps that supported the house was being pushed up by the roots and would eventually force itself through the floor. My mother became immobilized again. She didn't want anyone to know because someone knowing would mean being told what she knew already, that the tree was pushing the house over. Her only hope was if it rained there was a chance that the tree would get enough water and it would stop the ground from contracting and the house from shifting. She knew eventually she would have to decide between them, the house and the tree. The house, our safety, the past, and the only way she knew to have a future. And the tree, her husband, the past, and the only way she knew to have a future. Her way of dealing with it was to ignore it and hope it would go away.

Chapter 13

"Bless me, Father." I faltered. *I had been forced to repeat the* mantra so many times it had finally slipped.

"For I have sinned," the priest reminded me.

"For I have sinned," I repeated. "This is my first confession and these are all my sins."

There was a silence.

"This is all secret, isn't it?" I leaned in closer to the grill that separated us. It was Father Gillroy, the new priest, on the other side. He was very enthusiastic and made time in his life to smile.

"It is," he said.

I waited a bit longer, not sure what to say next. We'd been given a list of sins—arguing with your brothers and sisters, answering back, taking the name of the Lord in vain. I wanted to say, "All the things on the list, Father." But none of them was quite right. I didn't have sisters. I never answered back because I preferred to sulk. I didn't say "God" or "Jesus," I said "bloody hell." So I said, "I stayed up late."

"That's not a sin, my child."

"It might be," I said. "Because I was listening to my mother and she was talking to a man."

The outline of the priest on the other side of the grill flickered as he moved forward in his chair. "I'm sure that you did nothing wrong," he reassured me. "Just listening to your mother and a neighbor talking, I expect."

I could tell I had his attention now.

"A plumber," I said.

"Oh." He seemed relieved.

"But he'd finished the plumbing hours ago." I paused, remembering what had happened next. "Then she went to talk to Dad."

I connected with the priest's fishy eye, and I saw that he recognized me, so I said again: "This is all secret, isn't it?"

"Yes, of course. Only God is listening."

"Dad's in the tree; we go and talk to him there." I waited for my accolades. I assumed because of the angels in heaven and the Holy Spirit, I would be rewarded for having my own personal ghost. I felt so much better for telling him. Now I understood what this confession business was all about. I was working out things I hadn't understood before.

"In the tree?" the priest inquired. "How do you mean?"

"That's where we talk to him, since he died," I said.

I waited for the priest to ask for details, to give me my due praise. He didn't. The relief I'd felt moments earlier vanished and was replaced by red-faced embarrassment.

"Very good," he said. "Anything else to report?" I could tell he was trying to change the subject subtly and bring it back to my confession.

"I've done everything on the list," I blurted out.

He seemed happy enough with such a broad-spectrum admission.

"Say one perfect Hail Mary and one perfect Our Father and listen to the words as you say them."

And that was that. We'd been taught confession was just a little chat with you and the priest and God, and so it was. But it left me feeling peculiar. No one had said anything about that.

I knelt in the church, trying to ignore the fact that because I had taken so long in the confessional, there was now along the hallowed pews a row of girls, their heads dipped supposedly in prayer, whispering, "How many sins did you tell him?"

The crinkled up nose of Katherine Padley poked under the wall of my hair. "You're just supposed to do three or four off the list," she said.

"I know," I said. I felt indignant. "But I did the whole list."

She looked bewildered and wrinkled her nose up again; then she seemed to understand something that I didn't. She patted my arm in that special way the women at the funeral had done when they had supported the grieving family members under the elbow and led them to and from their seats in the church.

Chapter 14

"Is that your mother up the tree of a night?" Gladys asked me as I stepped up onto the table from the caramelized twirls on her living room carpet. She had already slipped the dress over my head. The weight of the beading caused it to sink with great speed over my body, like a stage curtain being dropped halfway through a performance. It had ballast, that dress, and a bizarre odor. Partly it smelled new, the seams, the thread, the edge left by the fresh cut of the scissors, but the overall fragrance was that of old ladies' clothes in the Saint Vincent de Paul shop. I was desperate to get out of it, but her question had come like all those adult questions did, when you least expected them.

"I've seen you all in the tree," she mumbled, pushing me up onto the table, a curve of pins poking out from her mouth. She looked at me with the lizard yellow of her eyes. I was too petrified to answer.

I heard the Neighborhood Watch sign on Gladys's gate shaking, then footsteps coming up her front stairs.

"Hello." There was a voice at the screen door. I'd never been more grateful for an interruption. Gladys's face folded into a question mark. She halted on the brink of one of the caramel twirls, where she was stopped dead like the grandfather's clock. All she had to do to see who was calling was take a step forward, but she hesitated for so long that the caller had to speak out again. Now that she was sure there was someone there, she limped with her square body to the screen door while I stayed on the table waiting.

"Father Gillroy." She breathed out, relieved, excited, and terrified all at once.

"On my rounds, Gladys, are you available?"

Gladys spluttered and muttered, spat out her mouthful of pins, and showed herself willing by initiating some hurried fumblings with the lock on the door.

"Look at the work in that, Gladys." Father Gillroy offered the compliment on seeing me standing on the kitchen table. He turned back to me. "You look lovely, Simone."

"Well, her mother asked . . . ," Gladys whispered to him. "She isn't up to it."

Father Gillroy nodded. If he was confused about why Gladys was making my communion dress months before I was due to wear it, he didn't show it.

That night the priest joined the long line of Misters who had come to call on us since Dad's death, seven months earlier. The other Misters had tips on accounts, wills, drains, and cookery, but the priest, in his Bermuda shorts and his bold patterned shirt with a gold cross pinned to the collar, had arrived with a new subcategory of advice: spiritual guidance. He came back with me across the hot road, and we found my mother in the space we mostly found her in those days; that was halfway through a number of domestic tasks—cooking, washing, cleaning, phoning. She would leave one for another, resume the previous, begin another, and do all of them badly. I knew she would be grabbing for her shoes when she heard the priest's sandaled feet slapping down the front path. She would be running in half-crescent swirls like the pattern on Gladys's carpet, worrying all at once about what to feed him, where to sit him, the inconvenience of it, the mess of the house.

She let us in, pushing Edward to the kitchen to cook something while she entertained the priest. She behaved as if she were being interviewed by an adoption agency, trying to present her best side, at the same time resentful that her suitability was being questioned. She was nervous, and scathing. It was childish, but at least she hadn't been hoisted into silence like the rest of us. The priest seemed aware that he inspired this response, but he projected over the awkwardness he was causing.

At least he wasn't dressed like a black crow, like the

old priest who had retired to the beach somewhere north and hot. His visits had been terrifying, a mystery they were, like weird performances where everyone had been rehearsed separately and brought together at the last minute, leaving all involved assuming the other party understood what was going on.

The young priest's style was more difficult to pigeon-hole because he wore normal clothes and talked about sports and gardening. He appeared to be like everyone else, but he wasn't because he was a priest. He accepted our hospitality on a take-it-or-leave-it basis, assuming he might be asked to leave or decide to go himself at any moment. Happy to eat or not eat, talk or sit in silence. But to give him his due, after a difficult meal of stew and rice—difficult because the stew was full of corn-flour lumps and the rice solid, and difficult because it was full of strangling silences—it was he, not my mother, that released us.

"Let them go off, Dawn, and get on with their homework."

We breathed as one, as silent a sigh of relief as we could, tiny, like a mouse's breath, and my mother and the priest retired to the veranda, where they sat opposite each other, Gerard wrapped around my mother's feet like a sleeping cat. They were drinking beer and talking easily it appeared from where I was half-hiding in the living room by the television.

"It's not like there's any question in her mind that he's there," I heard my mother say.

"I'm sure there isn't. The image is fascinating and not without symbolic significance. It's a form of thought transference."

"Huh?" My mother grunted.

The priest was overeducated but dim with lack of life experience, and my mother was clever but barely schooled.

"It's one way of explaining these types of experiences," he added.

"I wouldn't tell her that," my mother snapped. She was put out by the priest's explanation of who or what we talked to when we communicated with Dad. Not that she'd fessed up to the priest that she also partook of nightly rants in the tree with her dead husband.

"You transfer your thoughts, give them a voice, a persona," said the priest.

"She does. I don't," my mother cut in, speaking rather too defensively and giving herself away, I thought.

"Yes, 'she,' of course." The priest must have had an inkling of what was going on, but who'd told him? Gladys? She couldn't know. Vonnie? She would never say. Me in the confessional? That was supposed to be secret. Megan? I doubted it.

As they passed me on their way to the front door, they looked down on me, literally, lying as I was on the floor in front of the television. My mother shut the heavy glass door and collapsed onto the sofa behind me.

"I told him in confession," I finally admitted, wanting the weirdness in the air between us to disappear. I hoped I was saying the right thing.

"I gathered that," my mother said.

"They told us it was all a secret."

"He got to it in a roundabout way." She didn't look at me, she gazed up at the ceiling fan chopping its way through a crowd of flies that followed the slow blades. "He wondered if you still thought you could talk to your father."

I felt exposed and stupid. Why hadn't my mother stood up for me? Now she was acting as if it was all my problem, like she had never been involved. Like the whole thing was my own fantasy that she'd played no part in.

"It's like wish fulfillment," she said, as if explaining away what she and I both knew was real. But if she didn't believe anymore, why was she hiding the tree's path of destruction? Why didn't she call someone to look at the damage? I felt alone and ridiculous and without support.

"Go to bed," she said, dismissing everything we had been through together in the past few weeks. She stood up, and the anthem of the seven o'clock news played her out of the room.

Chapter 15

That night I wanted to hurt my little brother, Gerard, because I wanted to get to my mother. How could she abandon what she had believed in so strongly? It couldn't have been just pressure from a priest. Her relationship with religion had always been fickle. It had never involved going to church or believing in God. She had, however, believed that everything happened for a reason, until Dad had died; then she'd said that even that, the last wobbly cornerstone of her belief, had been knocked out. Anyway, it wasn't like her to be influenced or worried by what a priest thought. So I pinched Gerard hard three times in a row until he woke up crying.

I'd stood over him for ages getting up the guts to hurt him. He was asleep, I knew, because he was purring with such pleasure it was putting me off my attempts to sleep. But I wanted him to pay for my mother's betrayal, so I found a squidgy lump of skin on his arm, picked it up, and twisted. I felt bad, but nothing happened. I tried again.

This time he rolled over and murmured. By the third time I was feeling more desperate, so I squeezed harder and he sat up sharply, already crying.

"Daddy," he called, "Daddy," and I felt very badly.

I dived for my bed and landed on the pillow just as my mother arrived.

"Daddy," Gerard sobbed.

My mother took him in her arms and cuddled him close.

"What is it?" she kept asking.

"She pinched me." He pointed toward my bed and sobbed on.

"I didn't," I said. "He had a dream, and I can't get to sleep because he snores," I shouted. And the whole plan backfired because my mother took my little brother away to sleep with her. It suited both of them because it meant my mother had company in the bed she had been terrified to sleep in for the past weeks and my little brother got what we all wanted—to sleep in bed with our mother.

"Why do I have to sleep by myself?" I'd often queried. "You're older than me and you get to sleep with Dad and we have to sleep by ourselves. It's not fair."

She just said, "Go to bed." That was her answer because she didn't have an answer.

•   •   •

Then the back steps started to separate from the house, and we were finally forced to do something.

There was a gap between the house and the top step, and it was widening. The roots under the house had tightened their grip on the wooden stumps that held up the house, raising them. These had in turn raised a section of the house slightly and caused the steps to drop off. For the first week my mother just locked the back door and tied a rope across the bottom of the back steps and told us not to go near them. I had to use the front steps when I wanted to go and play with Megan. It was like the back part of the house was dead; it belonged now to the realm of the tree. I noticed also that the branches had grown to touch the house all along the back wall.

"Why don't you come down the back steps anymore?" Megan asked.

And Megan must have told her dad or her dad asked Megan why my mother was using the front steps to get to the laundry at the back of the house, so that night there was another Mister. It was odd to see Mr. King, a quiet, tuba-playing member of the Salvation Army, lifting the latch on the gate in the back fence and squeezing through the gap normally used only by us children.

He came to the back steps, saw the rope and the rift in the stairs, took a step back, and rerouted to the front of the house, parting the dusk as he moved, leaving a trail of slippery green air in his wake. Mother invited him in, and he sat at the kitchen table.

He'd never been in the house, he observed, not in all the years they'd been neighbors. There was no reason, he added. Mother agreed; she'd been in their house once, she thought, but that had been fifteen years ago.

He said, even though they'd known each other a long time, they didn't know each other that well, but because Megan and I were best friends, he wondered if he couldn't speak directly to her. He said he'd just seen the back steps and wondered if he couldn't help.

"I know someone who could come and look at the tree," he said.

My mother met Mr. King's gaze. We all waited to see what she would say. Edward's giant physics book slid off the sewing table, taking the snack he had concealed behind with it. It seemed no sooner had she appeased one neighbor than another one took up the torch.

"Clean that up," she yelled to Edward, redirecting her irritation.

"The tree, do you mean?" She turned back to Mr. King.

"Isn't that funny, you call me Mr. King and we've known each other sixteen years," he reflected. "Call me Andrew."

"I don't know if I can," she said. "I'll try." She took a breath. "I know it needs some attention, Andrew. I've got someone looking into it." She was dithering.

"I don't know how to approach this, and I think I'm probably going to do it badly," Mr. King said almost to himself, pausing for a moment before he plunged into what he knew was going to be a quagmire of barely held but deeply ingrained religious beliefs. "I don't begrudge your religion," he said. "And I try not to judge people by their God, but there seems to be a certain amount of superstition involved in your religion." A smirk it looked as if he wasn't expecting visited the edges of his lips.

I had no idea what the Salvation Army believed in, I thought they were just a brass band, I didn't know they had their own God as well.

My mother cocked her head; she didn't seem to have any idea what Mr. King was edging toward.

"Which I can't understand, but each to his own. Megan told me they'd climbed the tree the other night, and I was mad at her, but then she told me why." He shook his head slowly. "And I'm struggling with that. It's hard for one religion to accept another's, especially when it involves your own children's safety."

At which point my mother pulled Mr. King out of the house. They were standing on the front steps, a halo of moths diving into the porch light above their heads. I couldn't hear their conversation, but I guessed I was being betrayed again, and now I wished I'd never told anyone about the tree, not Megan, not my mother. Neither of them believed anyway, or they believed only when it was convenient for them. I hated them, but I didn't want to let them know how much I hated them; all I knew was that I would punish them through silence, that was the only response I knew to anything.

After Mr. King descended the front stairs in his black work shoes, my mother, who appeared to be working hard to convince him of something, tiptoed around me. That wasn't like her either. I decided she must be guilty or too weak to let people know what she believed, or maybe she didn't know what she believed.

Later that night, when the drain man arrived, taking the eight front steps in a single bound, I realized it wasn't that clear for her. She was confused about what she felt because it wasn't always convenient for her to have her dead husband in the tree outside her window. It sometimes helped, but the trouble it caused at other times, when the drain man arrived, for example, made it confusing.

Chapter 16

The first time I saw the drain man in our house, properly inside it, was that night, and he was too large to fit. He was as im- posing as Gulliver surrounded by the puny Lilliputians. It didn't feel right having him encased inside the walls; it felt like he would burst through the rotting seams of the house. Mother must have felt the same; I saw her cowering as he spoke. She led him out through the full-length win- dow in her bedroom to the veranda, but not before he'd lectured her about the state of the house and the tree and the roots and the steps.

"Dropping"—he flung an arm behind him, pointing to said steps—"dropping off the back of the house."

I stayed awake for hours, determined not to sleep so I could hear when the drain man left, if he left. I lay on my back so I couldn't get comfortable and kept one finger in my mouth, and every time I felt myself lowering into sleep, I bite my finger hard so I'd stay awake. With the added

noise of the tree rubbing at the window, it wasn't that difficult. I heard them stirring eventually, crouching down to
step through the window back into the house, then moving toward the front door. I knew Edward was still awake;
I could see him through my window bent over his books
but with half an ear listening as well.

He didn't see what I did, though, the two of them by
the front door in the shadows embracing. I hadn't meant
to but I had, and my mother was furious and shocked, and
I must have looked like the spy I was, standing in the
hallway not even trying to hide.

They kissed like people on television, and I must have
squealed because I was so cross I wanted to cry, but I had
paid my mother back, without realizing it, tenfold for be-
traying me to the priest and Mr. King.

Chapter 17

I crawled up the tree that night to commiserate with my dad. He sang me a lullaby I'd never heard before. It went over and over and soothed me to calmness. And to think I had believed, so stupidly I then realized, that because of the angels in heaven I'd been taught about I would be rewarded for finding my dad in the top of the tree. I thought it would be like Lourdes. People would journey from all over the world to our tree. They would make pilgrimages to be cured of their ailments. I fantasized about my fame, the fame of our house, our suburb. I didn't understand that you could be taught about the mystical but forbidden to believe in it, seek it out, or enjoy it. The mixed message caused a confusion to descend that made me hate the world, hate my mother, hate Megan and the drain man— my mother the most, though.

It hit me then that I only came to talk to my dead father when I felt lousy. When I felt good I ignored him.

"I'm so pleased to talk to you anytime in any condition," he answered.

I could see my mother in her bedroom window; she was looking straight up at us. I nested in behind a frayed drop of leaves. I knew she knew where I was, but I wasn't going back to the house, ever. I decided I was going to stay in the tree forever. I could come down to the lower branches to get food that I would ask Edward to bring me. And if I convinced him I needed it, maybe he could, with Mum's permission, build me a tree house a bit lower down. I could sleep in there. Really, there was no reason to return to earth.

I heard my mother hissing at me from below. She was stuck halfway out of her window. I refused to answer her.

"I'm furious with her," I said.

"She's got to get on and so do you," my father said.

He was so understanding, it made me cross. It was easy for him; it was so calm and peaceful where he was living, lit by the sunset in the salmon pink gaps between the branches. I wanted him to side with me, his only daughter, but he wouldn't, he was sitting on the confounded fence like he always had. He would never put me before her, and so discreetly he always put her before me.

"No way," I huffed. "No way."

My mother had woken Edward now, her henchman. They were on the top step; their voices transported easily through the balmy night air.

"Simone. Come down now," my mother said.

"No way, creeps," I replied.

It must have been after midnight. They advanced, Edward behind my mother. I could see him clutching the top of his pajama bottoms, trying to keep them from falling down. Any spring there may have been in the elastic waistband had been washed out long ago. Aware that the neighbors might be listening, Mum sent Edward out in front. She stayed back in the shadow of the laundry door. James was awake too, I could sense it. He was somewhere in the house watching.

I felt sorry for Edward having to do my mother's dirty work.

"No," I said when he was halfway up the tree, before he'd even said a word. "I'm not coming down, so you might as well not bother to come up."

"For God's sake, Simone," he said. "I need to go to bed. I've got exams tomorrow."

I remembered some elephantine aunt or other had commented on that, at the time of Dad's death: "and with Edward's exams coming up . . ."

"I'm not coming down ever," I said. "I hate you all and I'm going to live up here now."

"Why don't you start as of tomorrow?" said Edward. "And give me a break."

"No," I said.

"You're so bloody selfish," he said, retreating down the tree. But Mother wouldn't have it, and she demanded he climb up again.

"What's so good about this bloody tree?" he said, settling on a branch below mine, resigned it seemed to life in the tree with me.

"I can talk to Dad. That's all," I said. "And Mum used to, but now she doesn't anymore."

"What do you mean, talk to him? Dad's dead."

"You haven't even tried. So how would you know?"

"Because I know there's no point."

I wished he would, but I knew he was locked into the logic of his textbooks; he couldn't let go of that and I didn't hate him for it.

"I'm going to stay up here," I said. "Until she promises to stop kissing the plumber."

"Did she kiss him?"

"And not just a little kiss, either," I said.

"What else then?"

"It was like a kiss with arms."

I could see Edward shake his head. He seemed in no hurry to move now either.

"What is going on?" my mother called up. I could hear she was seething through the grille of her locked teeth. Neither of us answered her.

"Would one of you speak?" I heard a rustling below us and realized she had started to climb up after us.

"Where are you?" She had stopped at a point below Edward. Her voice was hoarse with restrained fury. She was trying to whisper, but I felt the entire neighborhood knew we were in the tree.

"Simone is upset," said Edward. "Because she saw you kissing the plumber."

Edward had taken up my corner, and I felt huge affection for him. My mother didn't reply.

"All I know is it's one o'clock and it's school tomorrow and I get in trouble from the teachers if you're tired," Mum finally said.

"Whose fault is that?" said Edward.

I couldn't remember him ever answering her back in that tone.

"I should be in bed," he said. "I've got exams tomorrow, but you wake me up like a madwoman and force me up this tree. I don't care if she stays up here or not."

Maybe because there was this distance and branches between us, Edward felt liberated to speak in a way he couldn't have face-to-face.

"It's none of your business what I do with the plumber," she said.

"It is, if you're kissing him," I said.

"Ssssh!" my mother hissed.

"And I don't want you to kiss him," I added.

Suddenly I became aware of this other silent person. The fourth party. The tree.

"You don't know," my mother said sounding feeble and close to tears. "I'm so lonely."

"How does that make us feel?" said Edward.

"See, you don't understand that I can love you, but still be lonely."

"You can talk to Dad," I said, speaking to the bark on the branch in front of where my chin was resting.

"I can talk to him, that's true, but I can't touch him."

"Imagine how he feels," I said.

"You're so on his side because he's dead. He's got such an unfair advantage!" She raised her voice.

She'd started to say that we would love him more than we loved her because of that. That he had died young, and missed out on decades of yelling at us. A job she now had to do exclusively. It gave her more wrinkles, she said, wrinkles that should have been shared out between the two of them, and it made us hate her more than him, that was her argument.

I don't know who moved first, but finally one of us did, and the others followed back on the ground. We stared at each other, then acted like nothing had really been said that had been said. But it was too late, it had been, and we slunk across the garden as a volley of mangoes fell from the tree in the Kings' backyard.

Chapter 18

Skirting around the house to the front steps, that's what we did all week, while Edward did his exams and we wondered what our mother would do with the house falling apart and the drain man's visits that were extending by half an hour on each occasion. The back door was now firmly shut. I didn't see Megan. I didn't stand by the back fence and call her, and she didn't call me. It was easy in that first week because school was finishing and we had exams too, but then we broke up, and normally before us would stretch seven golden weeks of sunshine and beach holidays and hours and hours playing with Megan. Not these holidays. There was no sign of anything normal.

On the last day of school Mrs. O'Grady, my teacher, found me under the school building hiding by the blackened stumps where the red soil was drilled with the holes of the ants' nests. I'd heard the school bell ring; it was three o'clock, time to go home, not for the day but for seven weeks.

I'd heard my class having their party on the floor above me. Believed I could smell the sugar from the pink icing on the fairy cakes I'd seen Katherine Padley bring in a large square Tupperware container. Of course our mother had forgotten we were supposed to contribute something to the party. I felt them treading on the boards above me, and in my cave I felt safe. After I'd heard the bell and the commotion as everyone dived for their bags and cleared their desks, I heard them run off. I peeked out from under the building. The gum trees rattled their leaves, and a gust of wind carried the scent of the eucalyptus down from the mountains; I felt there must be a storm coming.

Somewhere there was a rain-soaked eucalyptus forest. The school incinerator was burning the last of the year's rubbish, sending it into a brown funnel of smoke up to the never-ending blue. In the dry tufts of grass in front of me, I found a grass trap. Two lumps of grass tied in a double knot. Lethal if your foot landed in the trap when you were in full flight. Head over heels you could fly. I untied the trap I had seen Tommy Butler set for the teacher on play duty that lunchtime. As I untied it, I looked up and found myself staring at Mrs. O'Grady's kneecap.

I thought my absence had gone unnoticed, but I'd forgotten there was my desk and schoolbag giving me away,

and my mother had apparently been embarrassed into returning to the school with enough orange drink, diluted,
to go around the whole school. The container with my
name on it was hanging from Mrs. O'Grady's manicured
hand.

That was apparently when Mrs. O'Grady noticed I
was missing. She'd told my mother I was about—that is
actually how she'd put it. It was odd to hear that my
mother had been shamed into action, and I wasn't sure if
I was more embarrassed that she'd returned to the school
with a late contribution than if she'd dismissed it alto-
gether. Of course she was forgiven because of her husband's unexpected departure, and I could imagine there
was whispering in the staff room and those connections
reiterated.

Mrs. O'Grady led me back to the empty classroom
and sat at her desk while I collected my things.

"Thank you, Mrs. O'Grady," I said as I went to leave.

"Thank you, Simone. It's been a pleasure having you
in the class."

I stopped at the door. I didn't want to leave. Mrs.
O'Grady was pretty, and she wore a different dress every
day of the year. Her lipstick was pale pink, like an angel's
lips, and I knew she had no children and I dreamt she
would take me home. When I was in kindergarten I
thought the teachers lived there, but I had worked it out
now; they had their own houses, they didn't stay at school
overnight. I wanted to go to Mrs. O'Grady's house and not

mine. I knew she'd have a spare bed with clean sheets. I remembered then that I'd found a rock for her on the way to school that morning. I took it out and went up to her desk.

"Mrs. O'Grady." I handed her the smooth rock. I had realized when I picked it up how happy I was that I wasn't a rock, that I was a girl, and I could have been a rock, but I wasn't. It was smooth quartz.

"Thank you, Simone," she said. "I'll really treasure this."

And I don't know why, but I burst into tears. She pushed her chair out from her desk, and then her pale pink lips were talking in my ear. The same way they had done when she'd picked me out of the class the day my dad had died. The same way she'd consoled me on my first day back at school.

"It's a lot to ask a child to deal with." I think she was crying and speaking to herself.

"I don't want to go home," I said. "Please don't make me go."

She couldn't look at me or speak, she just held me and I cried.

"You'll have such a wonderful time . . ." She couldn't finish, because she knew I wouldn't have a wonderful holiday. I was condemned to seven weeks with my grieving mother and three brothers and a best friend I wasn't talking to.

Mrs. O'Grady didn't offer to drive me home. I wondered if it was because it would remind her too much of the day I had driven home with her to my house. My mother half insane at the door, telling me Dad was dead. They'd always known about his heart problem. They'd known since birth, since marriage, since children, but it made it no easier when, as had been predicted by the doctors all his life, he died at forty-three, at work.

I'd felt his heart once when it was fluttering. He'd move his head away from it as if he were trying to disown it. "Ticker's gone haywire again, Dawn," he'd say.

Sometimes people would ask how he was, and he would laugh. His merriment was infectious. "Not dead yet," he'd say.

It was the greatest joke ever. Not for Mum, she always looked worried. Dad didn't look worried, though, and now I knew why. If he died, which he did a few weeks later, it wasn't going to be his problem, it was going to be Mum's. I think he must have known he would soon be off the hook, floating away from us, having a marvelous time. There was not a second even for him to extract himself from life. When the time came, he just got up from the table and walked out the back door and never came back. Well, that's what it felt like. The clock just stopped, it didn't run down slowly. It just stopped.

He and his partner, Ab, had been moving a house, that's what they did. They found old Queenslanders often raised up high on wooden stumps, and they chopped them in half, sometimes quarters, loaded them onto semi-trailers, and drove them through the streets late at night to their new places of rest. All Dad's tools were still under our house. The long jacks they used to raise the houses from their stumps and his toolbox full of saws and hammers. There were parts of houses, twists of staircases, cornices from ceilings, sections of verandas, railing, half slabs of tongue-and-groove walls. All stacked and not moved since his death. Ab had promised he'd come and collect it all, but I knew he couldn't face us and Mum, and we couldn't face him or the prospect of losing the last bits of Dad. The bits that represented his work, the thing he loved, wooden houses and the idea that you could move them on the back of the truck—he never got over the novelty of that.

Couples would come to Dad and Ab's allotment and saunter along the corridors of houses bought on spec and choose their dream house. It always gave Dad a thrill, not just the business, what he loved was the life in these houses, often surrounded on all sides by verandas with full-length doors that opened out onto them.

"You're virtually living outside," he'd say. "With nature. In nature. That's pretty special. Beautiful houses. The best in the world."

He'd talked about the day when he would buy a block of land somewhere, then find the house with the widest veranda and move it there, in the dead of night, and rebuild it, bringing it back to life, that was the dream. His dream, not my mother's. She had no interest in what surrounded her; she was not house proud, she liked books and cigarettes and people and watching television.

Finally I walked out of school with my case full of books and the empty drink container. Up the hill I walked as slowly as I could, savoring every step of peace. The mountains at the back of the house held such promise. I wished I were a traveler. I could keep walking toward the line of lilac and green humps set against the ocean of sky. They were away, way beyond the drive-in movie and the monastery; the weekend before my mother had suddenly packed us all in the car and taken us there to confession. Something we rarely did, but Mother was superstitious, and I figured she needed to get something off her chest.

Below the mountains was Megan's school, with its amphitheater-shaped sports ground. She was probably at home already. Maybe she was calling for me. I quickened my pace.

When I got back I saw that Megan was already there, packing up the trailer with her father; they were leaving that afternoon to go on holiday. I watched from my bedroom window. The momentum caused by the possibility of travel seemed to fill them with such promise and energy, and the thought of staying put made me feel so dull.

We had slipped into a depression, we couldn't move. All we managed to do was mirror each other's moroseness. I caught Edward sneaking a look at the Kings' packing too. I mostly knew Edward as someone who sat behind a stack of books. Now that he was out from behind them, he didn't seem to know what to do with himself. His study had given him the perfect escape from Dad's death, but now the reality of it was beginning to touch him. He had no father, and not even any books.

James had actually worked up the guts—we'd dared him to do it when we'd met at the top of the hill on the way home from school—to ask Mum if we were going on holiday anywhere this year. The response he got was a deadly glare that seemed to indicate we'd be lucky to get even a trip into town.

Gerard couldn't care less; every day was a holiday for him, though these were his last days of innocence. The final weeks of freedom before he found out what it was like to have the precipice of returning to school hanging over you.

Chapter 19

Once Edward figured out that the summer break was long and there wasn't going to be a lot going on, he got a job in the supermarket stacking shelves. The rest of us watched television and ate peanut butter sandwiches from plastic picnic plates in front of the TV. Outside it was sweltering. The sky was blue, but we preferred to stay inside. If we couldn't go to the beach, we refused to commune with the world at all.

My mother objected for a few days, then gave in to the slovenliness. After all, when she yelled at us to play outside, she was usually hanging over a women's magazine, drinking a mug of soup. After a day or two she was slouched in front of the television with us watching the cricket. It was so boring, nothing happened for hours, but that matched our mood.

The cricket was slow, the heat made us slow. We lived on Weetbix and peanut butter sandwiches, and conveniently, as the Kings were away, we felt no guilt about not using the back of the house. We prayed for rain, we even went to church mainly for that reason, because my mother knew it was the only thing that would save our house, or that was the theory expounded by most of the Misters. We had been told that a tropical downpour would soak the earth and satisfy the thirsty roots of the tree and stop them interfering with the foundations of the house. Going to church to pray for the drenching was one superstitious step away from performing a rain dance in the back garden, and I half-expected Mum would do that too before the holidays were over.

There was one particularly bad day, I didn't know why at the time, but I realized much later that it was guilt, always guilt. There was stirring and murmurings at the base of the tree and some scratching and rustling in the night. We found our mother the next morning asleep by the trunk, laid out and pale. Was she dead or just asleep, or had she tripped over and knocked herself out? None of it seemed to add up to a satisfactory answer. We edged about the picture, trying to understand it. I leaned in to touch my mother's face, which was so pale it looked like an outline. Then I saw her move her fingers. She woke and sat bolt upright. "What's going on?" she asked in her usual sharp tone.

Once we realized that she was still alive and that this was just another of her outlandish responses to losing her husband, Edward mumbled something about being late for work and he was gone, up the side of the house he disappeared. And the three of us were left again with our mad mother and the horror of another empty, dry, blue, sunny day stretching before us.

The question What are you doing sleeping under the tree? didn't seem possible to ask her. It was so obvious but so impossible to contemplate. It was clear she had spent the night under the tree, and really we all knew why. The previous night I'd overheard her with the drain man; he was trying to convince her that the tree had to be cut down. The back steps were still out of action, and the floor near the back door was beginning to sag from the lack of support. Still my mother argued she wanted to wait.

"Wait for what?" The drain man had raised his voice.

The silence bore through the night. There was only the sound of Mr. Lu digging his series of trenches. Then I heard a wavering reply from my mother. "He's still with me."

I'd heard a set of keys jangling and the front door close; then his van started. I tried to analyze how he was feeling by the revs of the motor. Injured with underlying dull pain, the vibration of the engine seemed to say.

The next morning, my mother laid some keys in the center of the kitchen table. All day they sat in the middle of the table with no explanation of why these two keys joined by a twist of red-and-white twine had entered our house. There was an uncomfortable feeling around them. Gerard picked them up and started to play with them.

"Don't," my mother said. "You might, I don't know . . ." She took them off him.

"Why can't he have them?" I asked.

"Because they might break."

"What are they for?" I asked.

"They're just keys," my mother said angrily.

We discovered the next day driving to a mystery location that the keys were for a beach house at Tin Can Bay that was owned by the drain man, and that was where we were heading. We also discovered then that Mother had given the drain man permission to cut the tree down, hence the reason she had spent the night beneath the tree. Guilt. Always guilt.

We discovered all this driving up the highway with the late afternoon sun flickering on and off as we sped through a forest of pine trees. What was more shocking than that revelation was that the telling of it caused my mother to stop the car at a roadside stall selling pineapples and beg the woman there to let her into her farmhouse to use the phone. The three of us sat on the sofa for the rest of the afternoon while my mother attempted to find the drain man. When she finally did he was at our house, chain saw poised. Mum sobbed and pleaded with him to leave the tree where it was. He did.

Chapter 20

The beach house was like a long boat beached in a sandy thicket of emerald green pines. The needles filled the soil and poked into our feet as we approached, all barefoot after the six-and-a-half-hour drive. The pricking needles seemed a bad omen. They spiked our feet all the way across the sand trail that led to the house. There was a mailbox, 59 it had on it in white blocky letters, 59 Illana Drive. The drain man had written the address on a scrap of paper, and his writing appeared quite florid and learned-looking for a plumber, more like that of a book-keeper, I thought.

There were only three other houses in the forgotten street, but through the green mash of trees was the Pacific. From above, it appeared static, with some dancing white foam on top of the green-blue plate of water, and our longing to cast ourselves into the waves was powerful. We threw some things into the house—one room lined on each side with a row of unmade single beds—then we charged toward the sea. The temperature of the sand rose as we galloped through the scrub to the beach. Then the undergrowth ran out and the white sand took over and the heat soared and we dashed for the blue water, yelping and squealing.

To stand still would have caused our feet to blister. The water was rebirth, baptism, and heaven come to earth, and we played like seals for hours, piercing the waves with our bodies, then torpedoing toward the shore, our heads and shoulders figureheading the waves, steering them into the shallows, where we beached on our sides and allowed the waves to roll us over.

Our mother's limbs looked gloriously unknotted as she played with us for the first time since Dad's death. Squeezing with all her strength, she pinched the sides of an old plastic tube of suntan lotion she'd found in the bathroom, sending a jet of the stuff across the sand. In previous weeks this would have driven her into a rant, and we waited for her to begin, but instead she opened her mouth wide and laughed. The silence had been broken, the death between us was gone.

When the sun dropped behind the hill, we crouched in the twisted trees between the house and the beach. We spent most of our time in the bush between the pine trees and the long, block-shaped house. We ate outside, barbecuing everything—sausages, vegetables, even fruit was tossed onto the hot plate; bananas, tomatoes, pineapple, all were blackened on the fire.

It was so spidery in the house, we only went inside when we had to. More bugs would come out at night, seeking our reading lamps and smashing into the shades as they circled wildly. We met Edward from the bus and brought him back to show him all the hiding places we had found in the twisted trees. We watched him experience the scorching sand and the hot Pacific, our unconscious, our reason, our God. If we couldn't spear the waves, there was no point in living. Hours we spent in the stunted scrubs pretending to be soldiers waiting to ambush the enemy. We stayed there until it was dark, limping home only after the scarlet streaks of clouds had turned to gray, then black.

The drain man was there one day when we returned, sitting with my mother on the cement step at the front of the house. We formed a bewildered flank before them. It was us and them, and we weren't sure how we all fitted together; neither were they. My mother dithered, talked about feeding us for a long time before she pushed off from the cement step and headed in the direction of the kitchen. The drain man responded by driving three stumps into the prickling sand and handing Edward a cricket bat. We played on into the dark in a floodlit patch at the front of the house. None of us wanted to enjoy ourselves now, because it felt like such cold-blooded betrayal.

That was the first night they spent together under the stars on the beach, and I cried because Dad was four hundred and ninety miles away, connected by the same canopy of stars—I knew that—waiting for us to return and oblivious to all of it. His replacement had been so quick and brutal, and we evacuated the house the next morning with boxes of cereal and bottles of milk and swore to each other we were going to live in the stunted trees forever.

We hovered in the trees listening to the squawking of the giant gulls and the waves hissing below, then we heard their voices coming up the path from the beach. We stopped, still not sure what to do. For days we had been waiting to ambush somebody; now that there was someone to ambush we couldn't do it. Then Gerard called out, "Mum!" And dropped from the tree onto the path behind her. There was wailing and blood. He'd fallen onto a tree root, and a gash opened up in the bottom of his foot and the blood seeped out.

The crisis diverted the meaning of the moment, and somehow Edward and I ended up on either side of the bloody plot of sand. The others had all gone with Gerard to the bougainvillea-covered hospital. James wouldn't stay with us, he needed, he said, to be with Mum.

The drain man's presence had the opposite effect on us. Edward and I wanted so badly to not be anywhere near her. Also we wanted James to go with them to keep them separate. It was a telepathic plot. We'd looked at each other, Edward and I, and each known what the other was thinking. If they, our mother and the drain man, had just Gerard, they could pretend he was their child. They needed reminding there were four of us and that we would never be his family.

We crawled back into the trees. "He's the favorite," said Edward.

"Who?" I said.

"Gerard. Who else?"

"I thought James was," I said.

He was so unselfish, my mother was always saying. It would make me sigh and roll my eyes up to the fluorescent kitchen light.

"Gerard is," Edward repeated. "James was Dad's favorite."

"No," I said. "I was, wasn't I?"

"I dunno, I'm nobody's favorite."

"Yes you are," I said. "You're Mum's favorite."

"Who cares anyway?" he said. "Two more years anyway, then I can move out."

I knew he meant it. How would I ever see him again?

"Don't go," I said pathetically, as if the wishes of his creepy sister, as he called me, would make him stay. I was turning a flat rock over and over in my hand, wondering what it would take to make him stay. I couldn't contemplate living at home without Edward; I'd go with him. I couldn't live with my mother, that man, and my other two brothers.

We built a stone wall with the smooth rocks that poked out of the sand like lumps of butterscotch. Our medieval wall extended and curved to enclose some sheep we made with burrs from the eucalyptus bushes. I fantasized it was just us in the world working in the sand, creating a scene of early settlement. It soon deteriorated into a more abstract piling of the rocks, less functional, our medieval farm in the burning sand had been the starting point of our stone art. The second paddock lost its form, and the stone walls began to slide into other shapes—lines and squares and circles. It began to incorporate the scrubby trees. We tied grass around the lower branches. We climbed up to get some perspective on the area under construction. It was fragile work; it had the intricacies of a mosaic floor but no chance of that sort of permanence. We left it eventually, knowing it wouldn't be there the next day, but we accepted its fate. We had accomplished what we needed to do. We had fertilized this spot together and used the obsessiveness of creation to block out the real world.

Chapter 21

We returned home a week later and found the tree in our backyard was a burgeoning umbrella of lime green feathers, the roots now a complete hairy claw clutching at the foundations under the house. I sensed apprehension in the long grass that knocked in the wind against the wooden fence. A hoop of climbing rose had fallen from a rotting trellis that arched from the side of the house to the fence. The overgrownness had made the garden come alive. Dad didn't bother to inquire about our absence. There was no mention or inkling of any interest in where we'd been.

I could still feel the cushion of his affection holding me in the cup of the tree, but I felt the elastic between us was stretching, pulling us further apart. Also I felt he was more eager for my mother, and I was eager for him to want my mother. Or impatient for my mother to behave as she had when she'd first found him in the tree, when she had slept with the mattress of foliage by her side, when she had paced the base of the tree, when we had found her asleep by the trunk. I wanted to see that longing again because it had made me feel safe.

My mother walked out into the backyard. She had just seen the hairy claw under the house. She thrust her face up to the tree. I could feel her eyes searing through the leaves. The tree breathed, I felt it. It sighed, and she ran up the back stairs, forgetting how lethal they were, and she shut the door hard.

Then I saw the mule-like legs of Gladys, step, stepping down the drive, like a donkey picking its way along a stony path. Over her arm was the communion dress, the white of it muted by the dense green light radiating from the poinciana tree. Down the driveway she kept pick, picking. She stared up as she came into the backyard, into the realm of the tree, because the tree was a sight to behold.

It was like another life-form multiplying. The main root ran its course toward the house, and a smaller vein snaked away from the trunk toward the clothesline. Each finger of the tree's roots looked as if it could rub out any part of us, push out a wall, lift the clothesline, pluck us from the earth, curl a tentacle around us. It felt so thin, the house and its walls, like it would only take one surge from the tree to consume it. The tree had power and weight, and it was going to destroy us. Gladys looked shocked, amazed, furious, and satiated all at once.

I wanted to stop her going any further, but too late,

she donkey-stepped across the cracking path and I knew if Gladys saw any more, the claw under the house, we'd be doomed. There was complicity between us, and the drain man even, but if an outsider witnessed the damage, it would exist properly. I only then realized the severity of it. As Gladys's nose turned to the ground and followed the roots toward the house, I knew we were done for. She step, stepped closer to the house and dared to stretch her neck through the opening that led under the house. I could tell by the way her shoulders flexed back that she had seen the gnarled hand of the tree grabbing for the foundations. She had seen it all right and made it real.

By the time I got to the bottom of the tree, Gladys was gone. Mum caught sight of her tail as it disappeared around the edge of the garage. "What's that old hawk up to?" she said. Standing below her at the bottom of the steps, I pointed under the house to the evidence that proved our collective madness. The unbelievable sight of the tree's roots strangling the wooden stumps of the house.

"She saw," I said.

"I don't care," Mum replied, but I knew she did and she would when Gladys took whatever action it was I knew she would inevitably take.

Chapter 22

The house was disintegrating and so were we, but not without a party, Uncle Jack had said, when he came to stay from up north, where it was hot with snakes. He was tall and lean like a stick of sugarcane, with a merry smile and hands like wooden pallets.

"The house is falling down around you," he said. He'd come down to see a doctor about a crook knee.

"Drag them over," he said. "I want to see all the old girls. This may be my last chance. They can't have that many years left in them." So my mother went to the phone to ring all the old aunts.

When Jack saw what was going on under the house, he called out to Mum. He sat her down and told her they had to call someone immediately. She shook her head.

"We just need a little rain," she tried nervously. "That would shift things a bit."

"Shift things," he said. "What are you looking for, Dawn? A bloody miracle?"

"I don't know." Her voice was breathy.

Jack took all ten fingers and scratched his scalp with the irritation of it.

"I can't make any decisions about anything, right now," she said.

"I will if you don't," he said. "Dawn." He leaned forward. "Let me do this."

"No," she said. "Give me another day."

"What for?" he demanded.

"I need it." She looked him straight in the eye.

"You swear to me tomorrow you'll get someone out here or I'll cut that ruddy tree down myself."

She curled forward in her deck chair and dragged her knees up like a child. The rest of us breathed a sigh of relief, Uncle Jack was our savior. When the drain man had tried to be assertive, it had never worked, but he was too close and he was part of the problem. Jack could push in a different way, and we were so grateful. We were tipsy with his playful energy, light-headed with the relief that he seemed to have replaced the drain man, who hadn't been near the house since Jack arrived.

He pulled her out of the chair and pointed to where the floor had begun to sag by the back door. It wasn't difficult to imagine the weight of a foot forming a valley in the linoleum that could collapse into a deeper ravine and create a chasm that would fall through to the world out-side.

"I know." My mother sounded apologetic.

"I'm going to the timber yard tomorrow." Jack pulled my mother's knees back to the ground and tapped them with a long, slow hand.

"Thanks, Jack," she said.

And he did. He went to the mill the next day with Edward and they brought back a pile of wood and they nailed and sawed all day until the steps were braced and the floor at the back door reinforced.

Then in the late afternoon, just as the breeze began to blow in from the bay, scattering the smell of the newly sawn wood fixed to the back stairs, a taxi pulled up out-side. They were on schedule, all the old aunts. They stepped across the footpath gingerly, as if the blades of grass had been sharpened specifically to pierce the soles of their shoes. Then we noticed the reason for their cau-tion—they were all wearing heels, high heels! High heels for Uncle Jack. They were all in their eighties.

Auntie Mary, brittle boned and wily, who slept on a board like Uncle Fester, I always imagined, but without the nails. Aunt Cath, who wore a black eye patch and had her hair pulled back so tight in a silver bun I thought it would tear away from her scalp. Auntie Flo, an old trade unionist, and her husband, Uncle Val, the drunk.

They took up their seats at the kitchen table and remained there for hours, squashed together in the middle of the tremendous heat, drinking tea laced with slivers of brandy.

"How are you feeling at the moment?" they all took Mother to one side to ask her.

She bit back the tears for each of them and accepted a lacy hankie from Flo.

"The place is falling down," Uncle Jack reiterated as he took his cold beer out to the screen door at the top of the back steps.

"It's that tree," said Cath, looking over the top of her teacup, across the oval pond of murky brew lapping at her lips. "Chop it down, you'd get that much more light in here." Forever practical, Auntie Cath.

"She's right. It's that dark in here I can't think," said Mary.

"Can't think?" scoffed Flo.

"I can't see your lips, so I can't hear what you're saying."

"Put your hearing aid in," Flo teased her younger sister.

"I will if you put yours in."

"It shades the house, the tree does," said Flo. "It'd be hotter than hell in here without it."

"It'll pull the house over," said Cath, joining cup and saucer together. "You've got to do something, Dawn."

We all waited for Mother's reaction. She deflected confrontation by refilling the teapot. The steam hit her face, and she pulled back.

"I can't," she said, grinding the lid onto the pot. "It's where he is, in my mind. He's in the tree."

There was a beautiful silence, not awkward or uncomfortable, filled with minute sounds from the air that joined us, for they were all Irish, all Catholic, and all cursed with superstitious minds. They believed in ghosts, and if there was one in the tree, in their niece's backyard, so be it.

"I didn't think he'd go off to the other side that happily," said Cath, leaning over to the sink to toss the dregs of her tea out.

"He's not ready yet," said Mary. "And why should he be, I'm not either and I'm almost twice his age."

That was all for a few moments because they understood the dilemma utterly. On the one hand they were all of them perfectly pragmatic, not a sentimental bit of bone between them, so I thought surely house would win over tree. But then again, this was their niece's dead husband lingering on in an ancient tree. They shuffled their feet and downed their drinks. It was tricky.

Now that Jack understood the puzzle, he moseyed back to the screen door to take a fresh look at the problem. He stared for a few moments, then pointed down the twenty-two back steps into the back garden. "Who's that?"

"Who's what?" the old aunts chorused.

"There's some pensioner hovering in your backyard, Dawn."

They were on their feet, all the old girls, tottering around the edge of the kitchen table to take a look. The shuffling and the commotion so we could all fit at the back door and see what Jack was talking about was like a bunch of teenagers vying for the front row at a pop concert. I was being suspended in the middle of the scrum between the front row—my three aunts—and the back row—my mother, Uncle Jack, and the boys. It wasn't until I begged for some air that I was passed to the front and found myself pinned to the screen, somehow supported by the weight of them pushing from behind. Then I saw what they were all looking at—a group of strangers fanned around the base of the back steps.

Once my eyes refocused from the mesh of the screen a millimeter in front of me to the bottom of the steps, I realized it was the Neighborhood Watch women, headed by Gladys. They were taking turns peeking under the house to see the site of the potential destruction. The next thing, Mum pulled the door open, capturing me and the three aunts in one decisive moment and squashing us against the wall as she flung the door back so she could fly down the stairs, flapping her arms like a mad bird about to attack. On seeing the approach of my insane mother, the women parted, revealing for the first time that two official-looking men were inspecting the tree. One was bent over an electronic device pointed at the tree while the other measured the large root that ran in the direction of the house.

Uncle Jack took that as his cue to get involved. He opted, however, not to take any chances with the back steps and rushed through the house and down the front stairs.

What my mother couldn't believe was that they had assembled on the back lawn without permission. "You should have knocked," she said.

"We were just about to," Gladys spoke up.

"You weren't, you were snooping." My mother's neck and chin jutted forward like she was straining for an imaginary finishing line.

"Well, this affects all of us." Another of the Neighborhood Watch women stepped up beside Gladys.

"I'm sorry, madam, we didn't think anyone was home." It was one of the councilmen trying to explain their predicament.

"Well, we've been here all day. You should have knocked." Mum spoke straight back. The sparks were flying from her tongue. For ages they were arguing at the bottom of the steps before we all, one by one, made our way down. It took so long to move all the aunts to the backyard using the front steps. We had to find their walking sticks and guide them through the house, down the front steps, along the drive, over the cement block that led out of the garage, and finally into the back garden.

It was pensioners' showdown when we arrived. The two lines of old women faced each other. My mother was trapped in the center of it, and she ranted and raved and spun about angrily. The Neighborhood Watch women brayed and backed away and left the two councilmen to deal with my mother.

They stood for a long time, the two men taking turns to lean on one leg, then the other. It was true the house was falling down. That much they could verify, but there was nothing they could do, they reported to the assemblage. If the tree were on council land, then things would be different, but it wasn't, so maybe there was a case for health and safety, they could refer it on, that was all.

And the relief at not hearing the ultimatum she was expecting had an odd effect on my mother. I could tell that she was devastated. The decision had almost been taken out of her hands, but not quite. Her eyes looked empty. She must have imagined this showdown with the neighbors, but this wasn't the outcome she was anticipating. She would have expected to be told that the tree would have to go; then she'd be forced to cut it down and she could blame everyone but herself.

"Help," I wanted to yell as the two councilmen packed up and left.

"I didn't hear what they said." Mrs. Drummond looked bewildered.

"They can't make her cut it down." Mrs. Layton

mouthed the words out to her, overemphasizing the shape of each sound so Mrs. Drummond could hear.

Uncle Jack returned down the drive, having escorted the councilmen to their van. He dared to place himself between the files of opposing pensioners. My mother was dazed, as if a coconut had just landed on her head. She had only a gram of energy left, and with it she whispered to Jack. "Sort it out, Jack."

Not that it seemed Uncle Jack was waiting for her permission.

Chapter 23

"You know how we sort out a dispute like this up north?" Jack presented his rhetorical question with a lazy grin. They waited for the answer, the gathering of old women curving around Jack like an awakening smile.

"Get a pack of cards," he said to Mum.

Jack had taken center stage, and he was loving it.

"Choose your game," he challenged Gladys. His voice was as dry and flat as a northern riverbed.

I hoped he knew what he was doing. The column of rheumy eyes before him belonged to women with few passions other than cards and gossip.

"Bridge," said Gladys.

"Bridge it is." Jack nodded.

So our fate was to be decided by a deck of cards and a bottle of brandy.

"The winner is the winner," Jack said, outlining the rules. "And that'll be the end of it. If you lose, Dawn"—he threatened Mother with his bushy eyebrows—"you lose the tree."

My mother took a moment to accept the fact that the method of arbitration over this long-running dispute was to be a game of bridge. She nodded. Why not? It seemed fair. What other process could there be that was as just as a game of bridge?

"But if you lose"—he turned on Gladys, his monobrow signaling an equal warning—"you're to leave Dawn to decide her own fate. I know you'll keep your word."

"Of course," said Gladys, feigning offense and at the same time trying to find a loophole that might give her a second chance if she lost. I watched her mind work—best of three, she was thinking, but she didn't say it, I knew she was storing it.

"And that'll be the end of it," said Jack.

And so they shook on it, Jack, representing the interests of our family, and Gladys, heading the case for the neighborhood.

"Pair up then," said Jack. The family closed in around him, ready to discuss tactics, but this wasn't going to be a democratic process.

"Cath and Flo," said Jack, and he wrote their names down on the blackboard he'd sent Edward off to get from our room. I saw a necklace of flesh around Aunt Cath's throat tighten. She and Flo had fought for years. Jack was clever. He wasn't making this easy for anyone.

"Mary and Val," he wrote next. They hated each

other. They had been childhood sweethearts, but when
Mary outgrew Val and moved on to her next boyfriend,
Val only swapped sisters. He took up with Flo, and Mary
had never forgiven him for the lazy trade and Val had
never forgiven Mary for dumping him in the first place.

That left Jack and Mum, and their names were
chalked up. Mum was lousy at cards and could never sit
still long enough to finish a hand of poker. Jack, by con-
trast, was an artful player. He loved to play and he played
to win. He handed the chalk to Gladys.

Gladys claimed her long-term bridge partner, Daisy
Sanders. Mrs. Drummond, poker-backed and poker-
faced, was coupled with the crumpled Mrs. Layton, and
Mrs. Johnson, with her electric-shock hair, twirls of white
that stood on end, remained unmatched. They were short
a dowager. Who in the neighborhood could make up the
other pair? Vonnie's clothes trolley thundered down the
cement path on its way to the clothesline. All eyes
swiveled toward the back fence.

"Vonnie." They all spoke at once.

"Vonnie." A second later they were advancing down
the yard in a frightening flank.

"Vonnie," they called over the gray stump that connected the four gardens, the Kings', the Johnsons', Vonnie's, and ours.

"Fancy a game of bridge," they said, and Vonnie had
no idea what she was saying yes to.

Her face fell when Gladys informed her of the intention of the game, but it was too late, Vonnie's name was on the board beside that of her good neighbor Mrs. Johnson, and Vonnie knew where not to look. My mother's eyes were pleading with her to find an excuse to back out of the game. There was nothing she could do. Jack named the two teams, Us and Them.

"Hell couldn't be hotter," he said. "We'll play right here." And with a flick of the wrist he popped the four legs of the card table open.

Then there was a thought, I saw it pass between my mother and Vonnie. If Vonnie could sabotage her game . . . And that was that. A different demeanor engulfed my mother, and she flew about arranging chairs for the old aunts and finding stools for drinks.

"What if there is a gust of wind?" said Gladys, finding her own way of objecting to the location. "The cards could blow away. The game will be null and void and we'll have to start again."

"But shouldn't we play under the trophy, the very thing we're fighting for?" Jack's arm arched up toward the tree dramatically.

"Yes," our family, Us, all said.

If the tree could see our cards, everyone's cards, we must have thought collectively, surely it could intervene.

"No," said Them.

They were just as superstitious as Us. The tree was alive, it was an entity with a presence, not even a nihilist would contend that. And in their hatred of the tree they had also given it a persona, and they felt guilt at it having to witness its fate.

"All right," said Jack. "As you're the guests," he finally conceded, "you choose."

"House," said Gladys, and we began the long, slow haul back inside, leading the aunts through the garage and up the drive on their spiky heels.

"You know, they came out on a boat the size of a mattress," said Gladys, poking her nose in the direction of the Lus' backyard. "Had to fight off pirates. Missers told me. They had to eat all their jewelery."

"Gee they've had a rotten time," Mrs. Johnson chipped in.

"Bob had two of his toes off the other day," I heard Mrs. Drummond confide in Mrs. Sanders as I led my charge up the step into the garage.

"Is that from the diabetes?" Mrs. Sanders replied.

"No, just fell off. No circulation." Mrs. Drummond seemed quite pleased.

The neighborhood women were wary when they came to crossing our threshold; they must have been imagining victory, then the sticky issue of being surrounded by Us. We wouldn't make their exit easy, but Jack's presence must have assured Gladys fair play would prevail, because after her initial hesitation she stepped eagerly into the house. The rest of them were like sheep being herded through a gate; once one of them decided to go, the rest of them followed without thinking.

Things got off to a nervy start. Mum was drunk immediately on a lid full of sherry as the tables were being set up. Jack drew up the seating plan on the blackboard, and the kettle was on.

The first four sat at the card table under the ceiling fan (turned off at Gladys's request so as not to upset the cards). Another four around one end of the dining room table. And the last four sat in the kitchen under the harrowed and limp body of Jesus nailed to the cross.

Jack set the oven timer to ring every seven minutes; that was to be the time limit for each game. It was decided, because we were the home team, Us would move in a clockwise direction after each game and Them would stay where they were. Mum protested: our team was older and we were providing the booze and the venue, so we should stay put. A compromise was reached. After halftime they would change: Them would move and Us wouldn't. There would be twenty-four hands. Eighteen before the break and the remaining six afterward. All drinks other than water were banned until halftime, when they would stop to check the scores and have a toilet break. They were all under strict instructions from Jack to hold their bladders until then. So the drinking eased and the cards took over. No one was going to know until the end which side had won. The points would be counted and that would be that.

We watched, sitting on the carpet in the center of the room, intrigued for a few minutes, then thoroughly bored.

We made the mistake of switching on the television, and we were yelled at by ten women and two men.

"No," they said in unison.

It wasn't a great start for Us; the first four, under the fan in the living room, were Cath and Flo against Gladys and Daisy. Cath and Flo had barely spoken for thirty years but in a way that you would never know unless you knew. They were at every family do, they were sisters, and an outsider would assume they got on, but their relationship had been tarnished by a block of land that had been left to both sisters. Neither would agree to sell to the other or to cut the block in such a way that both had sea frontage. So the land had remained unused for thirty years, their dreams of an island retreat shattered by their own pig-headedness.

After losing the first hand to Gladys and Daisy Sanders, I saw them mumbling to each other. From that moment they were united, their iron jaws jutted from the rings of flesh on their necks. They wouldn't be beaten again. To see the two of them bonded over a common cause was uplifting.

I watched Vonnie win and win and win. She was desperate, I could see. I noticed from where I now sat sulking in the armchair beside her table that she was always dealt the best cards. Unlike the other players, I sneaked a look at their hands too; they varied, but Vonnie's were always superior. There was a streak of concern that divided her face. As good bridge players, they all knew who held every card in the deck. So for Vonnie to cheat would be impossible.

There was the silence and the shuffling, the cards being fanned and sorted, then the calls, deadpan—three diamonds, four spades—no eye contact, just these flat claims. It was a strange language, and it was deciding our future.

Jack rang the bell; we were halfway through.

"Time, ladies and gentlemen," he said, and we thrust open the doors and windows and turned the ceiling fan to maximum. The sun was boring onto the front wall of the house and roasting us alive.

"Not a breath of air," said Aunt Cath. "We've got to get a storm soon."

"Not tonight," said Aunt Mary as she pushed her chair out and headed for the loo. "Time to say a little prayer for Ireland."

The line at the toilet was long and boisterous. The ice had been broken, and it didn't feel like Us and Them; scores and hands were being discussed, tactics and the luck of the cards. It felt like there was deep affection between the teams. Jack was checking to see that everyone was happy, and Uncle Val was in his element, topping up the brandy glasses for those who were partaking and offering tea to those who weren't.

Then Uncle Jack turned his attention to the scores. Everything changed on the pronouncement of the totals. Them was winning by a few hundred points. Vonnie had the highest individual score, my mother the lowest. The challenge became real again, and they took their seats, arms folded, tying in their strength, ready for the last half.

The house was an oven. It was agreed the fan could be kept on low as long as it didn't unsettle the cards. The heat was taking its toll on all of them.

Then something altered; Vonnie started losing. I noticed she stopped being dealt good cards, and the tension rose in the Them team. Us could feel the slip, and the gap that opened up. It was like Us had stepped outside the game; they were no longer reacting to it, they were dictating it.

They could see the finish line, and they wanted to decide how they were going to cross it. They didn't need much, in fact it might as well be close, I could see them thinking. If they won by only a point, they would still win. And in some ways, the closer the finish the more irritating it would be for Gladys and her team.

It was sometime during the last game that my brothers and I realized Gerard was missing. No one saw him drift off. The drama before us was suddenly riveting as the result became more imminent.

The heat in the room was easing as the last hand was dealt. The sun was dropping, and the sky behind Gladys's green hedge was a variegated cocktail of orange and red.

The last cards were on the table, and the timer on the oven rang for the final time.

"Time," said Jack and he set about tallying the scores.

The room went quiet as my mother sighed and looked around. Something was wrong. And it was just as Uncle Jack announced that Us had won that my mother said, "Where's Gerard?"

"Best of three," said Gladys immediately.

"You agreed to the rules," said Jack. "And you agreed to abide by them."

"I think we should play on," said Gladys, trying to muster support from her teammates.

They shook their heads. "I'm happy with the result," said Mrs. Drummond. "We all played our best."

"Not everyone," said Gladys, turning to Vonnie. "You were on the wrong team." She accused Vonnie with her tarnished eyes.

"Where's Gerard?" said my mother again, ignoring Gladys.

No one knew.

"It's not a fair result." Gladys wasn't going to let it lie.

"Would you shut up?" said Mum. "Where is Gerard?"

We found the back door open and didn't think anything of it. Gerard would be downstairs playing on his scooter or up in the dirt under the house or in the yard rolling over in the grass. Or maybe he'd snuck through the Johnsons' fence to watch Mr. Lu digging his garden. No one expected to find anything else.

Chapter 24

When we saw him lying at the bottom of the tree in a heap, little Gerard, I was surprised how sick I felt. My mother screamed and ran to him, and Uncle Jack grabbed the phone.

Seeing her child twisted in a damaged ball was the last straw for my mother. She wailed and howled even after she'd discovered that he was alive. He would mend, but not my mother. Whatever had snapped inside her when she saw his body heaped at the bottom of the tree could never be fixed. And she was furious that she had been forced to come to that moment. In those slimmest seconds when she had believed him dead, the acid of that image had already burnt her guts, and by later that afternoon her clothes were hanging from her body. The weight seemed to have dropped off her in a few seconds.

She bellowed at the Neighborhood Watch women to leave. She cursed them for not wanting to play under the tree. She blamed them for his fall, for losing the game, for allowing her to win the tree she didn't want.

Her prize was above us, all around us, and she shouted at it like a madwoman until the ambulance arrived for Gerard and Jack took her under the house to calm her down. She yelled at everyone randomly, but mostly at the tree because she believed it had called to Gerard, beckoning him into its arms. His youngest, the delectable innocence, who could blame Dad for calling to Gerard and who could blame Gerard for seeking out his father?

I felt my stomach fizz when I saw his arm twisted back, bare white bone exposed, shattered and sharp like a broken teacup. I thought, Who will I fight with? Who will I poke when I'm feeling angry? I feared I would never do battle with Gerard again.

The Neighborhood Watch women moved up the drive in a wavering line that lapped toward the front gate as the ambulance arrived. I'd heard the siren coming, as I had months before when the fire truck came for me stuck in the tree, scooting down the main road, parting the traffic at the lights at the bottom of our hill. Then I saw the drain man's van flash by behind it. My mother saw it too. The longing and bewilderment came into her eyes, and the old aunts posted themselves at intervals around her, like a force field that was meant to keep her in and him out. All of them chattering and asking questions like a line of sparrows on the telephone wire. Twittering on about fractures and breaks, arthritis in later life. I wished someone would take an air rifle to them. Then suddenly they went quiet, their prattling hushed. They were monitoring her mood; she had gone into shock, and they tightened in around her.

The drain man was still waiting for her to signal him, to give him permission to open the door of his van and step down the drive, but she didn't. He must have seen the helix of old women around her and assumed it was one of them that was injured. The gravel crunched under the tires of his van, and he drove off as the ambulance men trotted down the drive carrying the stretcher.

The coil of relatives wrapped around my mother as an unwieldy mass. It moved with her wherever she went. It hung with her over Gerard as the ambulance men placed him on the stretcher. It hobbled up the hill with her to the back of the ambulance, which was where attempts were made to remove it, but there was no arguing with the aunts. They were as one, and they climbed in beside my mother and Gerard to protests from the ambulance men, saying it was against the law, there was no room, they just couldn't do it. All cautions were ignored, and the posse was locked in the back of the ambulance. It took hours at the other end to move that many old ladies in high heels up and down hospital corridors.

What happened to Gerard is that he broke his arm and his collarbone and he was unconscious, but he would be fine, he would mend. But not my mother, she was broken and possessed.

She came back from the hospital to find the drain man at the house. Jack had stayed with Auntie Cath at the hospital. Cath had fallen off her heels hobbling down a ramp and had been admitted for observation. With Jack absent, the drain man must have sensed an opening, but his timing, which had been so sensitive and impeccable to date, was way off the mark. My mother took one look at him and bawled that she never wanted to see him again. That was just her opener.

She followed it with "Or any man as long as I live."

He tried to defend himself. He'd seen the ambulance, he said, and he needed to know what was going on. It had worried him for the rest of the day not knowing.

I could see how difficult it was for her; she was touched by his concern, but she didn't want to allow herself to be.

"Go," she said. "And never come back. Ever! You make everything worse," she said, though her eyes said something different. Her eyes said confusion.

He left, the drain man, looking so defeated. For the first time I could remember, I felt sorry for him.

Her real anger, though, she held back for the tree. It was the sight of Gerard with his arm in a sling, his collarbone and ribs strapped, her perfect child damaged, that sent her back into a temper.

He was playing on the floor with the pile of toys he'd acquired over the day for his trouble; that triggered it.

There was a distant trembling of thunder, and the

clouds were gathering in the west. My mother's mood matched the brewing storm. The stirring, the rumbling. She had been holding something in that was near eruption. It was oozing around the corners of her sanity.

I heard her in the kitchen, in the cupboard under the sink, then in her bedroom, flinging open the cupboard doors and tearing garbage bags from a roll. She began to throw all his belongings into them. Last time they had been packed with tenderness into suitcases and boxes. This time they were hurled like rubbish. Now there was no order to the way she was doing it. Clothes, papers, books were all mixed together; nothing was going to be recycled or handed on, it was being treated as trash. She thumped around her bedroom and slammed the doors and drawers, making no secret of the fact that everything was going.

When she had finished and the garbage bags were brimming, two deep along her bedroom wall, the wind began to pick up, bringing with it the first sprays of rain. She moved through the house then, on the prowl, and glided down the back stairs. The weight in her movements increasing as she flung open the lid of Dad's toolbox. I heard the scraping of metal on cement. She was dragging the heavy head of the ax across the cracked cement floor and out into the garden. Then she picked it up and swung it at the trunk of the tree.

Inside we put our pillows over our heads and tried not

to listen to her while she bellowed at him at the top of her voice. She blamed him for what had happened to Gerard. The neighbors, everyone in the suburb, heard.

The drought broke that night, and between the cracks of thunder and the plops of rain we could hear her screaming at him. She accused him of taking her child, or trying to, of calling to him and forcing him to climb the tree. Then the neighborhood knew what the tree was about; if they hadn't before, they did now.

I couldn't bear it any longer. From my window I could see her taking wild swings at the tree with the ax. I was terrified of going near her in case she didn't know what she was doing. I started to shake. I was afraid she would kill me if I went too close.

I found Edward on the top step watching. We knew we had to get her inside. We called out to her.

"Mum . . . ," I tried first.

"Go away." She punched at my plea with an angry grunt.

We took a step back.

"Come on in, Mum . . . ," Edward tried next, sounding as normal as he could.

In the following silence we heard the ax drop. We could just make out her figure staggering into the strip of light my window cast on the backyard. Then we saw there was a shadow by her side. It was Vonnie, hovering over her like a great guardian angel. She was steering Mum away from the tree, toward the house. She led her up the back stairs and past us into the kitchen. At the same time Uncle Jack pushed open the front door.

"Just cut the stupid thing down," Edward yelled. He'd taken enough of her madness, he was finally blowing. "I'm going to if you don't." He stormed out of the kitchen and made for the back door.

"No," my mother screamed after him.

Uncle Jack went straight to Edward, directing him back to the kitchen.

"It's been a long day, troops," he said. He held Edward by the shoulders and spoke softly to his dark hair. "I suggest we all hit the sack and reconvene for a debrief at eleven hundred hours."

No one had any better suggestions, so we nodded and drifted our separate ways. Vonnie stayed on, though. I could hear her talking to my mother in her small, intense voice under the interrogating fluorescence of the kitchen light.

Chapter 25

Jack went back up north that week. He swore he would come again soon, but it had been five years since we'd seen him, not counting Dad's funeral, so I figured it would be five years till we saw him again. As he carried his bag out to the waiting taxi, we followed in a solemn file.

"Look after your mum." He spoke over his shoulder to Edward trailing just behind him. "Don't you give her any trouble, you two." He turned to James and me.

"And you, little fella"—he picked up Gerard and patted his tiny broken wing folded into his chest—"no more tree climbing." Gerard slid down Uncle Jack's side and dropped back to the grass on the footpath.

Jack wrapped his giant paw around Mum's back. "See ya, Dawn," he said.

Mum replied caustically, trying to hide how abandoned she felt by his departure.

"Yeah." She said it flatly to the grass at her feet.

"Remember, we have a deal," he reminded her.

The previous evening Jack had found the phone number of a tree surgeon. He had made the initial call and arranged for the man to ring my mother and agree on a date.

"I've told him to come within the week," said Jack.

"This week?" Mum protested. Then she nodded. "Yeah, all right," she added, trying to convince us all that she was ready now.

"What will it take?" Jack yelled at her. "He's lucky to be alive." I knew he meant Gerard.

Mum inspected the footpath as Jack told her off. He reduced her to age twelve.

"All right," she agreed, "I'll do it."

"Dawn!" He looked into her eyes.

"I hear you." She said it quietly, but there was meaning in the words.

"I'll call the cops if I hear you haven't cut it down." They were Uncle Jack's final words.

He said it in front of us, so we heard it too. I knew it was his crude way of letting us know that he didn't want us to feel like we were being deserted, which was exactly how we felt.

"I can't do all of it, Dawn. If I cut it down, you'll punish me forever," he said.

That was true enough. My mother could be bitter and irrational and Jack wasn't interested in the role of scapegoat. He was big enough to occupy the role, but he wasn't going to, even when our lives depended on it.

"You have to take the last step at least, Dawn," he said.

It was a long way down for Jack to stoop from the footpath to the cab. He threw his bag into the back and plunged down into the front seat next to the driver. Then he hauled the door closed. I thought he was looking at me as the taxi took off up the street, but I knew he had eyes like the Sacred Heart; they looked at everyone at the same time and followed you wherever you moved. We raced the taxi up the hill, but by the time we got to the hibiscus bushes it was pulling away from us. I stopped because I knew there was no point chasing it. I would never get Uncle Jack back now.

We drifted back to the house, all feeling lost. Mum was sinking her fury into the saucepan cupboard. She was crashing around like a Sherpa warding off the mountain spirits. An air of destitution sank over the dinner table that night; apart from Mum dropping plates on the table and Gerard asking for Uncle Jack, we sat in silence.

All the responsibility was with my mother again, and she exploded in the end. "Uncle Jack's got a family all right. He's someone else's father."

We knew he had a family that needed him, but we felt we needed him more.

Chapter 26

Uncle Jack rang late that night to check that we were all right; then he peppered every evening for the rest of the week with his phone calls, making sure my mother was going to do what she'd promised. We listened to her side of the telephone conversations and imagined Uncle Jack calling from his house in the middle of a hot sugarcane field in far north Queensland.

Eventually my mother did make the call, and a great hairy man came to our house with skid marks of green foliage staining his gray overalls and brown slivers of bark under his fingernails. He seemed nice enough, but we all kept our distance from him. We watched him from the back door walk a ring around his victim. And he eyed the tree up and down and said, "It'll be a shame to lose it."

We all nodded.

"But I understand," he said. "It has to be."

He would come the next weekend, Saturday morning, he said, if that suited. Yes, my mother replied, and the deal was done. Thanks be to God; my brothers and I all sighed, and I wondered if my father had heard the transaction.

"If she doesn't go through with it, I'll do it," Edward said.

"How?" James and I asked with legitimate interest, not knowing he was maybe just trying to sound big.

Edward gave James a sharp punch in the arm, and he pinched my leg hard. Even though James and I were both crying, it was a relief to be fighting again. Since Uncle Jack had left, the tension had been mounting between us. Gerard had found the three of us on the sofa the previous day, sitting close together. He didn't trust it, and he went and told on us and Mum yelled and sent us to our rooms. She'd assumed because we weren't arguing that we were up to something. We hadn't been. It wasn't that we were being friendly or plotting some misadventure, we were just too lost, too numb to fight.

Mum took us all to church that Sunday. Twice in the same month, I heard Mrs. Drummond comment, too deaf to know how loud her own voice was as Mum pushed us into a spare pew by the side altar. We were pleased, though, my brothers and I. I felt they were thinking the same thing I was—she's come to pray one last time for Dad's lost soul, a final beseeching before she gets rid of him.

Now beside her I saw my mother's prayer floating up to heaven. A tiny, bead-sized package, it made its way up a filigree finer and more magic than a spider's web, high up into the ceiling of the church. It continued its journey through the glass skylights toward heaven and God's ever-patient earpiece. Inside the package was a pearl, and on the pearl was inscribed her prayer.

It said, "God, tell me I have made the right decision—if you're there."

Even though the prayer disintegrated into a personal question of faith, there was a feeling of movement in her request that excited me.

I gave James and Edward a sideways look. The five of us were hunkered together along the pew like the losing team at a hockey match, but something was going to change; that was all we could hope for. Even if it was going to be for the worse, it would be better, because it would be different from how it was now. Static like a picture, like the world during the day waiting for the cool air from the sea to animate it, to lift its limbs and change its shape, anything now to create that wind that would move things and make it different.

She knew something was going to be taken if the tree didn't go; we all knew that, and it didn't feel to me like Dad was being cruel or terrible or acting like the cross father that he sometimes had been. The power of the tree and its encroachment on us felt more like the behavior of a child that suddenly grows up and doesn't know his own strength. Like a boy in the playground three heads taller than the rest of his classmates. It wasn't vindictive. Dad was just that frustrated boy with all that strength and nowhere to use it up. He wasn't being mean because he never had been. I knew that because my mother would criticize my father for being too generous. She would treat him like a criminal when she thought he had been unnecessarily kind to someone. It had never made sense, but she was jealous of his ability to want to share what he had.

It was still easier for them, my three brothers; for me there was more at stake. They had never talked to Dad in the tree. I was going to lose any chance I ever had of talking to him again, and I didn't know what I would do, exactly, without, at least, the chance of it.

Then a door slammed and the congregation jumped as one and the panes of orange glass in the side door that had blown closed shuddered. A tiny breeze had sprung up, and a crystal vase at the feet of Our Lady had toppled, and the gladioli fell like fiddlesticks at her feet.

Mrs. Beatty in the seat in front ran to rescue the vase and flowers, and her husband moved to fasten the door back. There was a breeze coming in from the bay. There had been no air, and the summer had been with us for months. The tropical fronts that could drop a dam load of water in an afternoon and ease the heat at the end of every day had still not arrived. So we were desperate to feel the air on our necks and to let it cool our heads at the roots of our hair. Sniff at it to see if it contained even a grain of water, but it didn't.

My mother thought, I felt her think it, that the wind was the mighty force of God, and she knew her prayers were answered. She had made the right decision.

Chapter 27

The next morning I woke to the curly call of the magpie. I opened an eye and saw through the dusty screens the wide blue sky and began my plans for the day. Then I remembered with a terrible thump in my guts that it was the first day back at school.

Our feet hated it, back in shoes after weeks of freedom. Itching seams and sleeves, confinement and words again. Still the rain hadn't come. It had started and stopped the night Mum had attacked the tree. It was unheard of. People were twitching and going mad waiting for the rain. Someone had been shot in a nearby suburb. A young father had started up his mower on a Sunday morning and the noise had sent his neighbor into a rage and he'd pulled a rifle from his cupboard and confronted him.

By the end of the week Megan and I had made up. We sat on our giant swing, each with one foot on the grass rocking us back and forward.

"Dinosaur followed by three little pigs," said Megan, thrusting her head back to see what she could read in the frothing clouds.

"There's a tiger I can see," I said. "And an old woman with only one eye."

"And a man on an emu." Megan pointed behind my head.

"We stayed in a house surrounded by sand," I said, turning to see if I could find the picture she described in the sky.

"We stayed up till late every night," said Megan. We both watched her man riding bareback across the sky on an emu.

"I wish we were always on holidays," she said. "Just forever at the beach."

I thought, I'm so glad we're not, but instead I said, "We've got a new teacher, Mrs. Britton, and she's got moles and bristles on her face."

"We've got Mr. Turnbull," said Megan.

"A man!" I said. I couldn't imagine that. I could barely conceive of anyone other than Mrs. O'Grady teaching me. I'd seen her that morning standing in front of her class, with her angel pink lips and her bedroom eyes heavy with pearl white eye shadow. We'd been lined up to go into church for first communion practice, so I could only admire her from afar.

Gerard had started school that day. I had to walk him

home. Mum was at the gate waiting for him, and he skipped the last bit home and ran into her arms.

"How was it?" she asked, and he didn't know how to answer.

"Can I have a drink?" he said.

"Of course you can," Mum answered.

I hurried past the hibiscus bushes full of grasshoppers, then I dawdled the last bit down the hill. I got lost staring through a frangipani tree into the dark space under the house behind the trees. It was an old Queenslander, the only one on our street, like the one I guessed where Ab had found Dad the day he died.

Ab had told Mum he thought it was a weird place for Dad to have a nap, under the veranda of the house they were moving. Then Ab had cried. I'd never seen a man cry. It looked so wrong, like it must really hurt. I had seen Dad shed a tear, though his tears had always been tears of joy and were somehow different. At the beach on a glorious day, he'd say, "God's own." He'd indicate the pallet of dark breakers before him and the moon rising over the dunes.

He was definitely the wrong person to die. It was God's mistake, Mum called it. A big mistake, and she spoke like she was going to get her revenge on God and take Him on somehow in a duel. I knew when I saw her looking up to the heavens that she was thinking, So that's your best shot? Like it hadn't crippled her. I could imagine my mother in the ring goading Him, a featherweight, light on her feet and mean, pitched against the Almighty but not frightened by Him at all.

I could see she was working it out, God was going to pay for this. My mother even suggested it, but never said it out loud, that Ab, a man with a nervous laugh to cover all occasions, should have been taken instead of our father.

I imagined Dad's last minutes under the dark veranda, blue light falling on him through the gaps in the veranda floor. He'd known how it would go in the end. His heart would flutter, then stop. It would gasp for breath like a fish hauled in and slapped on the deck; it would gasp and flap and finally stop.

Megan's foot pushed off the ground, and the swing rocked gently.

"Don't be surprised," I said to her, "if tomorrow morning you see a man with a beard in our backyard."

That was the only way I could tell Megan and remind myself that the date that my mother had organized with the tree man was almost upon us.

"Who is the man with the beard?" Megan asked.

"The man who is going to cut our tree down."

"Oh," Megan said.

Then we both saw it together. The decapitated head floating above us. That head looked so real, cut off at the neck, lying back on its mass of gray curls. It seemed a great crime had been committed somewhere in the heavens and we were witnessing the brutality of it and the head of the victim tumbling down to earth.

"Mozart!" I said. "It looks like Mozart."

"Or Beethoven," said Megan.

We looked around us. We couldn't believe the world wasn't stopping to gasp at the sight of this head rolling to earth. It lost none of its shape as it floated toward the horizon, not like other clouds that changed expressions, divided into parts, blew away in wisps. This cloud head stayed intact until it dropped below the line of houses, appearing as if it landed on their roofs and deflated like a punctured balloon.

Then the wind came in, the first hint of a storm, and a string of cloud rabbits raced with the speed of the mechanical ones they use at the dog track round and round the bottom of the sky.

We should have recognized the signs in the sky that day. We should have known it was an omen, that something was going to happen.

Heads don't roll across the sky like that for no reason, I remember thinking.

And the line of rabbits kept racing in a fading strip round the inside of the sky's great dome. Like a blue mixing bowl turned upside down, ringed with a pattern of racing bunnies.

The scraping of Mr. Lu's spade sounded heavier than it had all summer, like he was tired of his digging. The sun went behind a purple cloud, and the world went suddenly green.

"See you tomorrow," I said to Megan as I slipped through the gate in the fence.

Megan was already skipping down the path toward her house.

The drill of the cicadas slowed to a purr and the frog symphony began. There was a flurry of activity now it was dusk. Doors opened, sprinklers came to life, and across the fence Mrs. Lucas was dragging in her forgotten laundry.

With the cool came an explosion of sneezes as the changing wind affected the sinuses of the housewives of the suburb. There was a tightly packed chain of nasal blasts from Mrs. Lucas, a sort of "achar, achar, achar, achar."

Then a discharge from Mrs. Johnson that sounded like a bloodcurdling scream. It went on for minutes while every woman in the neighborhood cleared her nasal passages to adjust to the weather front.

You would have thought we would have recognized all these cues.

Chapter 28

But the first thing I heard that night was the rattle of rocks against the wall outside, right behind my head. They sprayed against the weatherboarding with such force I thought Megan's brother had fired them with his sling-shot. That woke me up, that and the door slamming as a gust of wind went through the house. I felt a fine spray on my face, the rain spraying against the window so hard it leaked around the edge of the frame. A wall of windows along the back of the house blasted closed in the next gust of wind, and that woke the rest of them. I stayed in bed a long time, listening to the wind and rain, trying to gauge their strength. The drought had broken, that much I knew.

I finally dared to look out the window into the back-yard. The tree was dancing, like a mad skeleton. Arching and folding in two with the force of the screaming wind. The branches were tugging at the power lines; they pulled and wrenched, straining them to their limit. A few attempts later the lines snapped, and their ends sprayed about in the dark air, hissing like a basket of live cobras. A second later the house plunged into darkness. All my fear jumped to my throat and I ran into Mum's room.

I heard my brothers too jumping from their beds and sprinting down the hall. They arrived by my mother's bed a second after me. Gerard was asleep in the bed beside her. Mother was already sitting up, listening to the howling wind; she had an ear turned toward it as if she was trying to decipher a meaning from its melancholy wailing.

"It's a cyclone," Edward tried to scream above the noise.

"It can't be, there wasn't any warning."

Not that any of us had listened to the news that night. It did explain, however, why I'd seen Mr. King clearing their garden, bringing the bins into the laundry, and tying down the swing.

"Did you listen to the news?" Edward asked.

"It's just a bad storm," Mum yelled back as a fresh pile of debris smashed against the side of the house and we dived for the floor. The wind seemed to have upped its strength in that one gust. It stayed at that pitch, screaming like a tortured cat, the life being twisted from its scrawny body.

The walls of the house sucked in, then out. I heard the first crack then. I thought it was the roof beginning to tear at the corner, but the noise came from the edge of the house.

We slid on our stomachs to the long window we used to crawl through to get to the veranda. I scrunched my eyes up and stared into the black, but there was nothing there. Then we realized why we couldn't see. The veranda had been torn from the side of the house. It went with a gust of wind and very little fuss, maybe assisted on its way by the lashing branches of the tree, now jumping in its place.

The room was illuminated for a brief second with a strobe of light, and we faced each other with terror. I had been hoping Mum would know what to do—tell us where to go, make it better, say things that would take away my fear—but in that brief flash of light I saw her fear was as great as ours. It was as if she was reading the thunder and the wind and it was relaying a message of terror and de-struction.

Without the buffer of the veranda between us and the tree, the branches began to knock against the wall of the house; there was nothing to keep them back. They punched and slapped at the weatherboarding.

"Come on," Edward screamed as another wave of tiles and fragments hit the outside wall. He knew we had to move to the other side of the house; we were in the direct path of the wind.

"No. Stay together," Mother demanded.

The branches were pounding the wall so violently that

the cupboard doors rattled open. Inside I saw all the garbage bags and boxes Mum had stacked on top of each other. All Dad's possessions she kept threatening to throw away—she had piled them back inside the cupboards.

I felt a vibration beneath my feet, and I lost my balance. The floor dropped an inch, then sprang back to meet us. I believed it was the roots that hugged the foundations of the house. It felt as if they were pulling at the stumps. The floor dropped again, and this time it didn't return to support us. All at once the windows blew out, and suddenly we were standing outside.

The doors of Mum's wardrobe blew away and the garbage bags began to spill open. Dad's clothes, his photographs, all his books and papers, everything he'd owned began to be sucked up into the sky. His fishing shirt filled and danced out into the night like a drunk jester. His flip-flops flew toward the only unbroken window left, shattering it on the way out. His golf clubs rolled across the floor and spiraled off into space. It was all released to the wind. I felt him leaving, taking his possessions with him. There was a system in the way it left. His newest possessions went first. Work clothes, papers, handkerchiefs, pajamas, tape recorder, cassette, then a line of photographs of us, of Mum, of his parents, all sucked out into the blackness. Then the things he had owned since he was a child; it all went in a kind of order.

We were glued to the spectacle. We watched until the

stream of possessions trickled down to the last few. As the final items escaped into the night, there was a flash of lightning. Through the smashed windows I saw Gladys's face at her door looking out at the chaos, her Neighborhood Watch sign spinning on her front gate like a Catherine wheel. I went to point it out to the others, but now it felt as if the whole room was being pulled away. It tipped again, the floor dropping out from under us.

I heard the crack then. It wasn't lightning. The sound was amplified so it vibrated in our bodies. It came from the room where we were standing, Mum's room; it was cracking off from the house. The bed was tipping with the floor. There was nothing between us and the black air swilling with spinning fragments.

"Get out," she yelled. She knew she had no time to save herself or to save Gerard.

We didn't know where to go. We only had a second. We headed toward an opening we could see as the floor gave way below us. Mother was torn between her escape and a sleeping Gerard. She chose Gerard—her life wouldn't have been worth living without him—and we leapt out of the room as the floor went and they slid away.

Chapter 29

We huddled together under the kitchen table with no idea where they were. In my mind they were together; Mum, Gerard, Dad, and his possessions, had all gone to the same place. I didn't know where. I knew they were all dead. For a while I sat with the feeling of being saved, but it didn't last long. It was soon overtaken by a peculiar pull, a feeling that it would be better to be with them than under the table with my brothers and the screeching wind. It was in the house now, gusting up and down the hallway. Jesus and his bruised heart were plucked from the wall above the fridge and spun off into the black space at the end of the hall. I was sickened by the wind, by the sound of it. It was unrelenting. It made me want to rant at it, scream for it to go away, because it felt like it had a center. It was some force personified, and it was playing with us.

We dared to come out from under the table. We went

to the back door to see if there was any trace of them. In the darkness I could see the earth at the base of the tree; it was billowing in and out, huffing and puffing as if the wind was coming from the center of the earth. The branches of the tree were like cracking whips, their ends flicking like angry cats' tails. We didn't speak to each other; there was no point, we wouldn't be heard above the screaming wind.

Then we somehow all agreed without speaking to open the back door. It flung into us with such force Edward was thrown back. We picked him up and pulled ourselves out of the house and joined the mad night. After our noiseless decision to look for them, we couldn't contain the silence, and we were screaming at each other because we knew we were going to die. We had no choice, even though I accepted already that they had been flung like Dad's possessions to a far corner of the world.

The wind was so strong our weight didn't seem enough to keep us planted on the stairs. My middle was being sucked back, then violently pushed forward. I knew if I let go of the railing I could be vacuumed up into the black air above us. Then in a sheet of white lightning we saw the mess, and the trees of the suburb arching like mad dancers, throwing their arms and cupping the air that was filled with flocks of bricks and wood and the Kings' laundry roof, which was being peeled off tile by tile. Across the fence we saw Vonnie's laundry door flip open like a gate on a cuckoo clock, and her clothes trolley flew out and was propelled down the path toward her clothesline unmanned.

The ground at the base of the tree was still swelling and bulging, then shrinking back like a burst balloon. As the air was sucked out, it choked like a dying breath, the skin of the earth then clinging tightly to the skeleton of the roots. It was more terrifying than the sound of wind. It felt like we stood between two never-ending high-speed trains.

We were at the bottom of the stairs sheltering just inside the laundry when we caught sight of part of Mum's room hooked on our back fence. To get to it we had to pass the tree. Logically there was no reason to visit the remains of the room, but we had no choice, we were driven toward it. We took a wide berth around the base of the tree, the branches flicking like a bully trying to whip you with his wet towel, and moved toward the carcass of the room.

You could see that it had once been a part of a room, but now it was a room from a dream, a dream come to life. We had stumbled upon a miracle, a vision, we thought, as we peered through the doorway, which was positioned sideways like a window. Inside we saw the bed tipped vertical and sheltered by an awning of wall. The bottom of it was jammed against our back fence, and there, lying in the bed, were Mum and Gerard. They lay side by side. The sheets were tied about them; they were bound to the bed like two mummies. Mum looked down, not that shocked to see us, and in her most deadpan voice, as matter-as-fact as a nurse taking a pulse, she said, "And that's why you should always tuck your sheets in."

As we peeled the bedding back and pulled them out, the walls around us began to vibrate and flap. The room was preparing to take off again. Another blast of wind and it would be lifted off into space and blown across the suburb.

We dived out into the rain that was now blowing horizontally into our faces, piercing our skin like darts, and we began our attempt to crawl back up the garden. Most of the debris was flying at head height. It was being torn off the houses, thrown into the air, then cascading like a waterfall down to the ground. A sheet of galvanized iron flew toward us. It was spinning and turning like a magic carpet out of control. Edward saw it first; it was heading for Mum and Gerard. He ran at them and pushed them to the ground. We watched it fly back up into the air, as if it was on a roller-coaster ride.

The shock of being almost decapitated awakened my mother. I could see it in her eyes as she picked Gerard up, struggled back to her feet, and made a dash for the house. James and I got to the back steps first. In the second we had before the others made it, I looked up to the missing piece of house. Where once Mum's room had nested, there were wooden stumps spiking the air, like the legs of a jetty that has been washed away. The tree was thrashing in the space the room had once occupied. All those tons of foliage the room had been holding back were free to lunge and flail in the extra space.

Then the wall of water was upon us. It must have swept down from the top of the hill and across the road. It took Mum's feet from under her and swept her and Gerard away. Edward yelled at us to stay on the steps as the bank of water kept coming. The garden was a lake, and they were gone.

Edward went after her, trying to find their bodies in the dark. He yelled and bashed the water with his hands. We watched helplessly from the steps as the water continued to flow out from under the house. It was getting deeper, rolling on to the Kings' backyard. Edward's call was furious, like an animal bellowing. He slapped the water again with his hands and tried to run, though he was waist deep.

I knew we would make it, the three of us, but Mum and Gerard were in danger; they were fragile and the storm was so angry I knew it wanted to take someone. It must have been a few seconds later when Mum emerged, but it felt like longer. She was spluttering and screaming; she had been swept down the yard to the back fence. There was no sign of Gerard. It was the first thing she called. "Where is he?"

There was nothing, only the howl of the wind.

She faced the tree and screamed, a bloodcurdling scream that cut through the wind. "Give him back!"

We all looked up then and saw that Gerard, arm still

in a cast and a sling, had been thrown into the branches of the tree; he was clinging on like a bush baby. The branch waved about, threatening to drop him into the water.

Edward hesitated before climbing past the bubbling pool of water at the bottom of the tree. It was boiling over like a mud pool, sending up jets as the ground belched and the hollow under the tumulus took in tons of water. Mum was trying to haul herself back to the house, but she had no strength left. There was nothing to hold on to, and she was a terrible swimmer. James ran into the house and ripped the sheets from his bed. We tried to tie them together to throw out to her, but we wouldn't have had the strength to pull her in.

My mother's relief at being rescued from her bed, then surviving the sheet of iron that almost tore her head off, was turning now to exhausted fury. She yelled at the storm, she wouldn't be taken. She dared it to try, or to take any of us for that matter.

The lightning and thunder were so violent; they had been insignificant compared to the strength of the wind, but now they were matching it. There was no time between them; I tried to count the gap in elephants—one elephant, two elephant. It was only a few seconds.

The tree was moving too; not only was it lashing its branches at Edward and Gerard as they tried to escape but the base of it was shifting. The wind had loosened the earth around the base, and the water filled the cavity. It was lifting the tree higher into the sky.

Edward was swimming away from it. I thought they were going to be pulled down into the grabbing tentacles of its roots. Gerard was spluttering as he surfaced for a moment. He was dragged underwater by Edward, so desperate to get away. It felt like a Bible story in a suburban backyard, like the woman who turned to salt or the babbling tower that split apart or the Red Sea parting. I didn't know which one, but it had that strength. Edward got to Mum and hauled her, still raging, toward the steps.

Dad said he had to leave her now. He said it was time for him to go.

I heard it. I don't know how. I just heard it inside my head.

She answered him. She never wanted to see him again. He was a menace, he was stopping her life. I heard that as well, though all she said was "Go."

"Go," she called into the wind. "Go."

With her final scream came an explosion. The noise was not familiar; it was mechanical, filled with twisting roots and cracking wood. The tree was unearthed, it was falling. With great majesty it began to drop. It fell toward the missing room, slamming at last onto the wooden stumps, its branches splayed out like two long arms. The great root ball at its base was levered out, and the roots fanned like Medusa's hair slippery with snakes.

The torrent of water kept sliding down the hill. The next wave came, carrying Dad's toolbox. High in the water it floated off down the yard, followed by his workbench, the jacks he used to move his houses, his old hat and gloves—they all flowed on a great wave that cleared the back fence and headed out into the suburb. The bed unsnagged from the back fence and went too, all of it floating down the hill toward the creek. I imagined it flowing on as the rain continued. From there into the river. And I dreamt all night of its path as we slept under the dining room table. I saw it join up with Dad's clothes, his photographs, his papers, his gardening shirt, I saw everything amass at the mouth of the river, then empty out into the bay, where it dispersed and was gone forever. All the possessions that represented a life—a hat, a shirt, some photographs, bits of wood and tools, and Dad was gone.

Chapter 30

Gerard remembers very little of what happened. It is the wind and the water we all recall. The water that finally carried him away, that collected up his belongings the wind had scattered and brought them all together. The possessions floating down the waterways; the bed, the tools, the clothes, making a final tour of the town where he lived all his life and coming to rest in his beloved bay.

Gerard doesn't remember flying through the air on a bed or being found in the ruins of the room in the backyard or being flung into the tree or half-drowned as he was dragged by Edward back to the house. His memory, as is all of ours, is of the wind and the river.

Mum was thirty-seven then, and I believe it was her instinct for the drama of life that saved her. If she'd closed down, she wouldn't have lived, she would have gone with him. But in the end she was prepared to go only so far. She was willing to enter the odd arena of their supernatural relationship, but she kept a part of one foot on the ground, in the real world.

She'd had a reprieve from his death, been able to stretch out his departure, but the storm, which came almost a year to the day after he died, forced Mum to choose which road she was going to take.

Finally she had to choose between life and death, between him and the drain man. In my imagination he had even been offering to allow her to bring Gerard as well. He asked her three times: first sailing across her garden on a bed that had been sucked out of her bedroom. Then as the sheet of iron flew toward her, then as the tidal wave swept her away. Each time tested her will to live, to fight for life and for her family. Maybe he had felt her wavering before that, and had sensed a glitch in her will to live, a weakness for the past, for what had been. But each time she reassured him she wasn't going with him. He couldn't take her, and the struggle strengthened her will to live. By the time she got to top of the steps, she had lost three lives, but she had won. She had made her decision.

"Go," she yelled. "I'm staying here." And she slammed the door on him.

If I'm ever asked what love is, I think that. To consider giving up your precious place in life, for someone else, for love. But I never tell people about all this, because I know they would laugh and think I was mad or making it up.

For a long time I never heard anything from Dad, or maybe I knew we had to get on with living too. Mum and

I had both been somewhere in between. I blocked him out after that, stopped thinking about him, assumed now he was really dead and gone, my relationship with my father had finished. I'd had a father for ten years, now I didn't, so in one way you could see it as one less parent to worry about. I locked him out, buried him in the anty soil again and mostly forgot about him. I felt guilt about pretending he wasn't so important, and sometimes I didn't like not knowing where he was. He'd always been in the tree, and when the tree went I assumed that was the last I'd ever hear from my father.

Sometimes the memory of him would surface, and it would terrify me. He would appear to me as a skeleton, or as a sick man, too weak to live, one who had deserted us. I would even go so far as to say I hated him. I was so angry that he had died, and my only way of dealing with it was to decide he was really gone. I didn't know then—how could I, I was only ten—that you have your parents for life, even if you've never met them. Whether they're dead or alive, they're around for good in you. What a curse it is having to know death so young, but to fear it makes truly living impossible.

Chapter 31

I woke the morning after the storm sardined under the kitchen table. James's toes were in my face, and beyond was my mother's back, then Gerard. We crawled out, desperate to see how the world had changed in the wake of the storm. We rushed to the back door. The first thing that struck us was the terrifying space left by the tree. It was lying like a lazy drunk across the garden. It had crushed the fences around us; we had no boundaries holding us in. I knew that in one way we were free.

The wind was still strong; you could lean into it and feel as if it were holding you up. Water poured from under the house in a brown stream that gushed across the road from the Lombardellis' and raced down our hill and through the Kings' yard, eventually joining up with the storm water drains that ran down to the creek.

All the houses of the suburb stretched before us in a grid; they lay bare and exposed. I'd never noticed how square the blocks were before. The square houses with their square lawns, now with patches missing, walls that had disappeared, roofs blown away, fences crushed, cars and trailers turned over. Then I realized why the landscape was so open and why up on the hill the whispering trees at the monastery had changed shape. The trees of the suburb were bare; they had been stripped of their leaves. I followed the line of destruction from the horizon to our backyard, stopping for a moment at the Kings' house, where Mr. King was already stretching a tarpaulin across a gaping hole in the laundry roof. Then I saw our swing twisted in its frame; the rope securing it had broken and the carriage had been free to thrash loose in the frame. I had to climb through the branches of the tree sprawled across our entire backyard to get to it.

Megan was there already, standing in the cage of the bent swing.

"Dad says he can fix it," she said.

"Will he?" I asked. I couldn't imagine life without it.

"He reckons he will." She was distracted by something behind me.

"Wow," she said, seeing the tree lying in my mother's missing bedroom.

"Mum was in there with Gerard," I said. "When it got ripped off."

Megan's mouth dropped open, and she took in a little gasp of breath. "Are they, you know?"

"Nah," I said.

Her amazement was short-lived. "Did you hear about Mr. Lucas?" she said. "He was on the loo when their roof tore off."

It was my turn to open my mouth.

This was the first of the storm stories that whizzed around the neighborhood at a speed similar to that of the cyclone itself.

Everyone had their own disaster. We found Gladys wandering around on her front step. "My grandfather was struck by lightning," she said, roaming through the wreckage in her garden. "Was thirsty for the rest of his life," she said, trying to make sense of a ball of debris caught up in her front fence.

"That's the roof off the Lucases' loo," my mum exclaimed.

"The trouble it caused." Gladys was dithering. We assumed she was referring to the storm. "We were forever up and down getting him glasses of water." The rest of us had moved on, but Gladys was still stuck on her grandfather. "He had a terrible thirst. The mess. The mess." She was shaking her head now and pointing to her front gate and the missing sign.

"Someone stole it." She shook her finger at the scandalous world. "I wired that sign to the gate myself."

The fact that the gate itself had twisted from its hinges and lay battered on her footpath didn't give her a clue as to the fate of the sign, proved how keen she was to believe in crime and violation before all else. I didn't have the heart to tell her that we'd seen the sign spinning off her gate and heading for outer space.

We waded back to our house, weaving our way through the branches of the fallen tree. Vonnie was at the end of her path retrieving her upturned clothes trolley.

"I needed a new one anyway," she said with the same dry delivery my mother had used when we found her in her bed in the backyard. It was housewives' resignation mixed with a philosopher's perception. Not downtrodden, a kind of Zen knowledge and acceptance that when things happen, they happen for a reason.

Then Gladys nodded toward the Lus' back garden, delivering a strange look of awe as if it was the stable in Bethlehem and she'd just seen the birth of the baby Jesus.

"Have you seen?" she asked.

"No," we said dumbly, craning our necks over the fence to see what she was hinting at. Then we saw the reason for her reverence. The Lus' back garden had been transformed into a rice paddy. The trenches Mr. Lu had been digging all summer had filled with water and saved the low-set house from flooding. We crawled through the hole in the Johnsons' fence to get a better look. Buddha was sitting on his altar, peacefully looking over the calm waters. Another Bible story sprang to mind as I watched a school of fish shoot off across the rice field. Was it the story of the women with the lamps and the oil? I wasn't sure. I just knew it felt biblical.

Mr. Lu came out carrying a fishing rod. "Hello. Hello," he called excitedly.

We watched him hand the fishing rod to Buddha.

Chapter 32

The sky still appeared bruised with the remnants of the tropical front when the drain man arrived. His square red truck with the caged-in tray rolled to a stop outside our house. He surveyed the damage from the cabin, taking note of the empty room, the fallen tree, and with some relief my mother's mood as she came across the road to him. There was intensity in their greeting. This is it, my brothers and I thought, this is going to be our future. Our mother will be skipping out with the drain man. It wasn't better, it wasn't worse, we had no control over anything, that was all I remember thinking.

It took us the entire day to clear away the tree. Gradually, as the hours wore on and more of the branches were removed, the space opened up before us and we were all intrigued by the view. You could see the streets of trees striped bare to the horizon, the jacarandas and the frangi-

pani and a gum two blocks away full of lorikeets screaming. Still we felt self-conscious without our green cloak to
shield us. It would take us a long time to get used to the
open space left by the tree. The view was one thing—we
could even see the sun set now—but the gap left by the
tree, symbolic and otherwise, we felt in many ways. We
were on show now; everyone was watching us to see what
we would do next.

The devastation of our house seemed too much in the
beginning. The idea that no matter what, even if your father died, you were always safe in your own house, that
security was gone too. It represented more pain and another death.

There was emptiness in our lives now that we had
managed to put off for a year. Even for Edward and
James, who had never really believed in Dad's presence
in the tree, because we had, we had kept him alive for
them.

Gerard and I went with Mum and the drain man on
one last trip to the dump. She felt scrawny, my mum, I remember thinking that, as I slid along the seat in the front
of the drain man's truck to sit beside her. I felt bigger than
she; she was so frail, I wanted to pick her up like one of my
old dolls and wrap her in a blanket. We drove through the
streets of devastation.

Along the river the picture was different. The water
had taken whole houses. The scenes were more bizarre, a

trailer halfway up a tree and dead animals ebbing in the floodwaters. The roads were rivers, and people were rowing along them as if they were in a Venetian canal.

Then we saw our bearded tree man, cutting his way through a jacaranda that had fallen across a street. We waved to him, but he was busy slicing a corridor through the trunk to create a passage wide enough for cars to get through. Now he didn't appear so like the grim reaper with a chain saw for a scythe. He was a Samaritan now, helping the unfortunate victims. I wondered if he even remembered he had a date at our house. Maybe he would call round later and see that his job had been done.

"When are we getting the next storm?" Gerard asked excitedly, unaware of the anguish on people's faces and the smell of death in the air.

We rattled down the hill into the dump. The man stationed in the corrugated iron shed waved us in, then ushered us along the aisles of junk to where the rest of the tree lay dying in the wet heat. We jumped out and watched the drain man maneuver the truck back and lift the tray. The logs clattered down and joined the heap of tree.

The drain man jumped down from the truck and joined the dump man. They stood apart from us, the dump man scuffing his work boots in the orange earth, watching my mother. Mum was standing by the tree having a cigarette, farewelling the giant that had been with us for all my life.

The significance of the moment was lost on Gerard

and me. We were chasing each other over the pile of wood, our feet skating out from under us as the logs rolled and slid. Mum was so preoccupied she didn't even bother to yell at us. She threw her cigarette into the dust and squashed the life out of it with the heel of her shoe.

Chapter 33

In many ways I was relieved he was gone, not bothering me
anymore, lingering outside my window, calling me in the
middle of the night. I collected butterflies and played with
Megan, and most of the time I was happy. Then something
would happen, some unexpected emotion would jump on
me as I rounded a new corner in life, and the feelings
would leak out and sometimes it was difficult to dam
them back in.

Seeing Katherine Padley's father at my first communion, that set me off. It was the way he took this photograph of her, like she was the most beautiful and the most
clever girl in the class. I wanted that, and I howled so
much I went red and ugly to the point where even my
mother became embarrassed, and she was never one to
worry about causing a scene. She had to drag me out of
the church I was howling so loudly, gulping and gasping

with despair. I had no idea where the noises were coming from.

So I stood with my mother in the ladies' room with tears coursing down my face and her trying everything to hold them back. She tried to repair me, but these were tears from the pit, from that far below they raced to the surface and burst forth in their own form. She was wiping my face, a red blotch of sadness. She wasn't used to other people's outbursts, just her own. She didn't know how to act. She tried being nice, being reasonable, affectionate, understanding, manipulative; then at the end of her repertoire, when all else had failed, she did anger.

"Stop it," she screeched so loudly the entire congregation must have heard. "Just stop, Simone." She was trying to be strict with me as another puppy yelp escaped unexpectedly from my stomach. It was hurting, the tears were coming from so low down.

"You've got to pull yourself together and go in there and hold your head high."

She had no ability to deal with another person's pain. Her own dramas were the most important thing, even when someone else needed to have one.

By the time I got back to the church, my body was only sometimes shuddering from the center. Mum looked at me sternly, as if that would stop the movement, but I had no control over it. She pushed me off in the direction of the altar, and I took my seat beside Katherine Padley.

She patted my arm, like she had the day I'd spent too long in the confessional. I sighed, knowing the whole congregation felt sorry for me. I hated that. I read their thoughts. Poor girl, no dad.

I have no recollection of the ceremony, of what happens at a first communion. I remember there were envelopes from all the old aunts with money in them, and from Uncle Jack. And that by some miracle the first communion dress Gladys had made for me was shredded in the storm by glass from a falling window. It seemed that fabric was never meant to marry, man or God, Gladys said.

I remember looking in a mirror at the great drops of water clinging to my face and my mother trying to hold them back and reconstruct me. And my mother then choosing a hymn from Dad's funeral to cry to. It was as if she had to compete for the drama prize after my breakdown. It was her turn then to be led from the church.

We'd both recovered by the time the professional photographer arrived. He wasn't anyone's dad. He was being paid to take our picture, so he treated us all the same. I felt as if I looked like a million dollars by then, dressed as one of God's little angels. But the photograph stands testament to this day; in it I look like I only half-belonged. My mother was having a cigarette around the back of the vestry; she'd gone without one for a few hours, and the trauma of having to deal with my raw emotions, then hers, was too much. My three brothers, as brothers should, could have cared less.

Then I went back to the way I remained for years, with no idea when or why the feelings would overtake me. That was because I was suspended in deep freeze. Trapped in a gaseous fog in a glass beaker, like some experiment from my brother's chemistry class.

Chapter 34

You would have thought, we all did, now the third point of the triangle had been rubbed out, that my mother would have taken up with the drain man without fear or guilt. No one would have blamed her; she was thirty-seven and still bony, wild, and attractive. But when the tree was gone, so was her desire to be with the drain man. They were all part of the same structure. He belonged in the same equation as Dad, and when Dad was removed the sum fell apart.

My mother had used them both, in a strange way. Her relationship with the drain man allowed her to keep a part of herself in the land of the living. He was the balance, the opposite; that was his attraction. He possessed everything my father did not. But when Dad left, the drain man had no counterpoint. He was just a man, a mortal. What had seemed like superhuman power before became very mundane. He was just alive and, compared to being dead, it wasn't that interesting.

I doubt if my mother was conscious of this; we certainly weren't. It was only years later that I understood. She never talked about it, how they finished, but I remember the night. It was a few weeks after the storm, and we assumed she was leaving a respectable gap between Dad and taking up permanently with the drain man. The phone rang; it was him, I could tell by the way she kicked her shoes off while she was talking to him and dragged the phone into her room like a teenager. She sat on the bed and entwined her legs while she pulled the telephone cord through her fingers.

The four of us were watching television; it was a Friday night, one of the last Edward spent with us. He had just shaved for the first time, not that he had a lot of reason to, but he was impatient to move on to the next phase of his life, the world of aftershave and girls. For him the answer to the last year was looking forward, not back. I wish I could have done the same.

We all slumped, knowing what the phone call meant: Mum was going to take up with the drain man and our lives would be over. Immediately we started arguing over a bottle of Coke and some bags of chips. She got off the phone, said she was going out, and went straight to the bathroom, yelling through the door at Edward for leaving such a mess and using her razor. Not long afterward the drain man arrived. He sat on the sofa beside me while Mum was coloring her mouth in with red lipstick. I was so exhausted, I couldn't move.

"What's on, guys?" he said, not at all nervous. I thought we were within our rights to expect him to show some fear or anxiety at taking over from our father, but he didn't. I thought, You cocky bastard, think you can just walk in here and take our mother away from us. I said nothing else, neither did he. Then nothing for fifteen minutes; we watched the television in silence. When the program finished and there was still no sign of her, he went off to see what was wrong. That felt like pure antagonism. How did he get the right to go into the bathroom to see if our own mother was all right? Of course she wasn't. She was on the floor clutching her lipstick. She couldn't do it. They didn't end up going anywhere. They sat on the floor in her room instead, drinking beer.

Her room was a building site, there was no veranda, no windows, but there were four walls and a roof and a mattress on the floor. The romantic aspect of the room didn't escape us. There was no electricity in there, so they lit a candle and burnt it onto a plate. We waited up, assuming this was my mother's last episode of regret and remorse before they actually spent the night together in our house. We had accepted the inevitability of it; we all wondered how long it would be until we were forced to meet his children at some hideous suburban beer garden.

Then an odd thing happened, he left. There were no dramatics from my mother, she wasn't yelling after him and throwing bottles. There was shuffling at the front door as she maybe kissed him before he left. But I'd learnt the sound of a long passionate kiss and a short perfunctory peck, and this was the latter.

I was lying in my bed running for joy, my legs cycling through the covers. He's dumped her, I thought. Gone back to his wife. They always do, according to my mother. But it wasn't the case; my mother had called it off.

We couldn't believe the attraction between them had just died. They had a look about them when they were together, they were meant to be. We had prepared ourselves for a stepfather. Then when it didn't happen, when she called it off—we couldn't believe our luck. We kept thinking the next weekend he would show up, then the next weekend, that maybe she would change her mind and call him, but she didn't. In the months to come, I shocked myself, I changed my mind, I prayed he would come around again because my mother was as miserable as sin.

But we eventually realized he wasn't coming back. With the death of the tree had come the death of my mother's feelings for the drain man. The silence seemed to fall on her, and I hated seeing such a passionate woman frozen in her stride. Sometimes it would fire out of her and she would be mad and crazy and yell at us and dress in purple for a week, but a lot of the time she was just normal, life's most hideous crime.

That was the end of that era. Life wasn't always full of grief, sometimes we forgot him for ages, occasionally we were torn apart by the memory of him, then it would go away and in time return sporadically, just like an old friend.

Chapter 35

And it all went on, life for everyone. There was no death anywhere, making Dad's death even more irregular. Eighty-year-old aunts had their jubilees and gold and silver and ruby celebrations, and friends' parents became grandparents, and it seemed nobody died anymore. I actually longed to see death again, thinking that if I could watch it, someone else's demise, then I could understand it. Or maybe it would remove the pain of my father's death. But everyone seemed immortal.

Occasionally I thought, One parent down, only one to go. And I suspected my mother wouldn't die for a long time. She'd live on like a woolly mammoth so I wouldn't have to go through the grim affair of her death until I was so much older that I hoped I wouldn't care as much. And the sky that had appeared to open and take my father away was eventually sewn up again where it had torn apart. The jagged seam mended, and the sky became the vast blue above that represented the possibility in a life that anything could happen.

Then secondary school came and I was desperate to re-define myself, not to be the girl whose father had died. I dreamt of going away to school where no one had borne witness to my past, but there was no money for that, so I spent my secondary school with all the girls who limited, I felt, who I was and kept me trapped in that identity. I longed to be described as something else—the smart girl, the girl who was good at swimming, even the bad girl or the girl who smoked and went off with boys. But I was forever the sad girl whose father had died; that identity was propped up by everyone.

I don't know if my brothers had the same problem. They went off to different schools, where they became known by their last name. Even Gerard the baby grew up and became O'Neill. I asked what they were called if they were in the playground, for example, and the teacher wanted to single them out. If someone called "O'Neill," and they both responded, then it was "Not you, O'Neill. You! O'Neill!" And they'd point to the particular O'Neill they were after. Their first names were never used. My brothers didn't think this was funny or unusual.

After the first budding freedom of escaping the strait-jacket of school, I remained somehow living along life, outside the gates of the city. I was always drawn to people who were missing a loved one, sometimes even a limb. It was a great curiosity to me to know people with both parents; they, to me, had everything.

I had so few memories of my father, and either my mother didn't want to share hers or she didn't have any, and I didn't have enough to go round. My brothers were similar. Edward had drinking insights, recollections of Dad at football matches or being shown how to knot a tie or make a dovetail joint. Nothing that helped me.

I was looking for something broader, an image of him as a person rather than as a father.

"What's your strongest memory of Dad?" I asked James from a standing start, no warning at all that I was about to knife through niceties straight to the personal.

"I've only got the vaguest memory of you in all of it," I said.

"I remember not existing," he said. "Not feeling like I was wholly on earth," he said. The words could have been mine.

That was the oddest thing. James had always felt like me, thought like me, but I'd ignored him, I suppose for that reason. I was more interested in what Edward thought and how much Gerard knew, and as my mother was always the focus, we all had relationships with her that somehow precluded relationships with each other.

There was an anger toward my mother—all four of us had it, all for different reasons. It would still cement us when we were together and she wasn't there. It was our intimacy, our unexpressed anger at her. We could recall plotting against her, trying to poison her at one point with something from Edward's chemistry set, but it was bright green, so she knew immediately there was something wrong. We had mixed it with lime green drink, which she never drank anyway, so we gave her that warning, but she swore she was going to call the cops and get us all put in a children's home.

She still floated above it all, my mother, usually wearing something no one would ever consider wearing, but somehow pulling it off. Even though Dad's death had happened a long time ago, there was a part of all of us resentful and lost in the thin walls of that house. We were all of us a bit indistinct. But sometimes I was as angry as I'd been when she betrayed me to the priest and Mr. King. It was the pain and hurt of a ten-year-old. I thought the boys were immune to it, but I saw glimpses of their anger.

Once we met for a picnic, the whole family. My mother was still as thin as a post, with very little interest in food, but obsessed that everyone else should eat.

"Get a sausage for the kids," Mum yelled over to Edward, who was turning the blackened crescents on the portable barbecue. He waved his tongs in my direction. I grinned back at the sight of him sweating over the hot plate. The smoke twisting up through the gray, rattling foliage of the scraggly gums to the heavens above. Then I noticed him stack a plate of food and pass it to our mother.

I saw it; everyone seemed to except Edward. It was a

plate of charcoaled food, the scrag end of everything. Gerard found it very amusing. "Mate, that's burnt to buggery," he said.

And I saw Edward's face. He looked awful. And he'd thought he loved her, I could see him thinking. If he did, why had he passed her a plate of inedible food?

"Sorry, Mum," he said.

And Mum raised an eyebrow of acknowledgment in his direction to let him know she understood the symbolism of it.

That day she snapped at James as well. He often treated her like a child, patronized her if she got a word or a fact wrong.

"Don't treat me like an imbecile, because I'm not one and if I am one, so are you," she finally said.

And I saw James have to tunnel into himself to find out what his problem was. She had no time or etiquette for helping us work out our anger. She was angry too, she said. It was a fact of life. It didn't stop us wishing she could be a little more helpful though.

I had my own score to settle with her. We'd agreed to meet, but it had to be somewhere neutral, I thought. Somewhere without domestic distraction, I said. Not that either of us was interested in domestic detail, but we would have the excuse of it, if it was there.

I wanted an apology. I don't know what for. I just knew I felt I deserved one, for having to be her daughter, like every mother should apologize for her behavior, for her choices, for what she did and didn't do. I was prepared to apologize too for being an adolescent, and this was the moment I had chosen to do it. I was hoping my mother knew this, that she could read my mind.

We met up a mountain above the heat of the suburbs that stretched out to the sea below us. We sat in the cool rain forest, the whipbirds—not the crows and sparrows of the suburbs, but the cracking call of the whipbird—and the tinkling of the bellbird punctuating our conversation and the picture of the suburb below. It was our inescapable identity card. It was a peculiar meeting because we each wanted something from it, to take away to start anew, a resolution to begin again.

My mother had arrived dramatically. The car was overheating, she was lucky to make it up the hill. What did we have to meet up here for? Her eccentricities, which had always amused me, had, over the years, begun to grate.

It was her idea, I reminded her.

Now, looking at each other, we couldn't remember the reason for the meeting. To see each other, to exchange snapshots of our past, our version of it, but why now? Why not last year or the year before? I didn't know.

"What was Dad like?" I asked, not knowing I was going to. My mother wasn't fazed, didn't stop to take it in or hammer the importance of the moment home by leaving a long pause.

"Oh, I don't know," she said.

"You do."

"I don't. I've almost forgotten him."

"No you haven't," I said.

"I've tried to forget him, and I've spent so long doing it, it's almost worked."

I tried again. "What was he like when he was young?" I asked.

"You've seen pictures," she said.

"I've seen pictures, yes, but was he, I don't know, funny, happy?"

"He was like you."

That was all I got out of her, but it helped somehow.

"Tell me again how you met him," I said.

"They," she started, referring her gaze to the suburbs below, "your father and Ab, moved a house onto the block next door and I made them a cup of tea and that was that."

I'd heard it before, but I loved the feelings the description gave me. I'd invented the picture of that day. The house brushing the trees as it came down the street, bumping up over the gutter. My mother watching with her mother as half a house floated past the window.

"Did Gran say make them a cup of tea?" I asked.

"No way, I saw your father and said, I'll take them in a cup of tea."

It was a powerful portrait for me, my parents' meeting. Their eyes seeing each other for the first time. In the netherworld, four children are already waiting to parachute to earth to join them.

From the hindsight of the mountain I could see the fences and boundaries of the suburb below. I could escape geographically, but not mentally. I could be angry with my mother, throw things at her and yell at her, demand that she apologize or that she read my mind, but it wouldn't change the fundamental problem that she was not my father, and that was what the problem was.

I didn't know that all I wanted, all I needed was my father's love. I didn't know why I didn't know it, why someone couldn't tell me. First that I could have it, and second that my mother wasn't going to give it to me. It has taken me such a long time to work that out. The years of pain, trapped in my foggy beaker.

Slowly then, over time, my feeling toward my mother softened and she became what she always had been to me—my mother. I realized I was asking for something I couldn't have. I couldn't have a father's love from a mother or the other way around. People were separate, and I had to accept that sometimes you don't get the other, or you have it for ten years, or ten days, and you have to make that enough to last for a lifetime. But you can't get the same love from anyone else. And it ruins your life if you try. That was a liberation for me, learning that finally, but it came a long, long time later. I learned this, and that some roles remain unfilled.

Chapter 36

Many years after that I called on my father again. I don't know why, still no one else had died. I hadn't even been able to expunge my grief for him at someone else's funeral.

I don't know what made me decide I needed to talk to him. It was the anniversary of his death, and I went to his grave. I said, "Sorry."

"Don't be," he said.

"But I've shut you out, forgotten you, left you for dead."

"You have to, and you're here now."

"I'm an opportunist," I said. I don't know why I said that.

"Love your mother," he said. "She's a good woman."

"I know," I said, over and over again. "I know, I know, I know. I just regress when I see her. I become ten."

"Next time see if you can be eleven."

Instead of flowers, I left a pile of sodden tissues on his grave.

•   •   •

It seems a long time ago that I was rocking back and forth on that swing with Megan, not a care in the world apart from which figures were sprinting past in the raw blue above. That is a million miles away, almost. If every day is one hundred miles, then every year is thirty-six thousand, five hundred miles, then twenty years is seven hundred and thirty thousand miles away, not a million, but a long way.

But the past is a place I like to visit, and the clouds are still in my life in massive formations. Sometimes they appear in layers that contain everyone's lives and everyone's stories. I see my own as well in great layers, and they make me think of Megan and how we could compare our stories in the cloud friezes. My story would be contained in hers and hers in mine. The story of the tree would be in there, but from both perspectives. I miss the freedom though of interpreting the clouds with her from our great swing and the freedom of being a child at dusk.

Over the years I've noticed the eccentricities surface in all four of us. We all lay dormant in our pupae until later life. It wasn't until then that we all allowed ourselves to take up the gift of freedom that our mother had demonstrated to us daily. They all have their own stories, my three brothers, and I can't tell them for them. We have talked about the tree and what it meant, but it has been gone a long time, and now there is a brash eucalyptus in its place.

They've never really said why they wouldn't climb the tree and talk to Dad. That all remains unsaid. I knew it embarrassed them at the time and they didn't believe it, or if they did they would never admit it or act on it. James might have, I thought on a desperate day, but it would have been like saying a prayer out of habit or hope, even when you don't believe in God.

Edward has the most children, and it's not a Catholic thing, he just has a lot of children and they all have perfect teeth. Gerard unexpectedly took over Dad's business from Ab and has made a great success of it. James was a late starter, later even than me because he wandered the world for many years.

"Thursday's child," my mother would always say, "has far to go."

He joined a religious sect for a while. Mum went to rescue him from somewhere in France. I imagine her pulling him out by the ear, as if he was still eight years old. They got on a plane, and she brought him back. She didn't even go into Paris. None of us could believe that.

"Why would I want to?" she said. "That's not what I went for, is it? I went to get your damned brother back."

Still, all wasn't squared with God, or at least that's how I felt my mother saw things. If she'd felt even with Him there wouldn't be this anger. Since Dad's death she had shaken her fist at Him symbolically and promised to get back at Him.

It was two Christians who bore the brunt of her

grudge. She couldn't take Him on in the ring, so she had to pay back some of His disciples.

There were words at her front door apparently the day she opened it and found the two women on the top step. Words along the lines of God being unreliable and a shoddy excuse, open to any interpretation that took your fancy. The two Christians took it well by all accounts. Then there was a push and much evidence debated in the courtroom as to whether a foot was placed inside the threshold before or after my mother attacked. She paid the price though, my mother, for closing the door on the foot of one of the women. It wouldn't have been such a bad injury but the woman was wearing sandals and she broke her ankle and her foot in several places.

Mr. Lombardelli was a key witness at the trial. He was just passing on his way to lawn bowls, and he saw the whole shocking scene. My mother wasn't ever convicted, there wasn't enough evidence, but the shock of it was terrible.

Chapter 37

About the same time, Mum turned fifty-five, and she said she'd come to the end of her time in the suburbs and she sold the house. We hated her for doing that. We couldn't believe she could be so selfish, but we knew it was time for her to move on. She had outgrown it and so had we. The eucalyptus that had been planted in place of the poinciana had always looked a desperate substitute. All the memories were with us anyway, deep inside, we didn't need the house anymore. We didn't know that then, though; we cajoled and objected and tried to work out reasons why she should keep it. She was retiring, she said, and moving to the beach, up north.

"It's not some geriatric, shopping mall shithole," she said. "Like old people seem drawn to."

"What are you going to do there?" I asked.

"How should I know?" she answered.

"You won't know anyone."

"So, I'll meet people."

I was just trying to put her off.

She was right, though. It was a little settlement, old and untouched, just south of where we had spent that summer holiday after Dad had died. And she met him again, the drain man, after eighteen years. It was a casual thing at first. They'd never stopped thinking about each other in all those years. They hadn't kept in touch, but each always knew through acquaintances what the other was up to. They met at the end of a jetty where they both were fishing. My mother is a great fisherwoman. She loves the fight.

It began as just the two of them going on fishing excursions out to the bay, then as the months went on we realized it was more serious. When I first saw him again in the driveway of Mum's house, I cried; the great welting sobs returned. It reminded me of what my dad would have looked like if he was still alive. He would have been similar, not that old, still young enough to have his health and his retirement. Why, why, I thought as I sobbed, eighteen years after his death, did he have to go so young? It was hard to explain my tears to my mother and the drain man, but they knew. The drain man was still Dad's replacement, even after all those years.

They live together now in a beach house surrounded by hibiscus bushes full of grasshoppers. The drain man's name is George, but we call him Hunk, because he still is.

It's not like a normal love affair, the type you get used

to hearing about. They are two deeply attractive souls engaged in the dynamic struggle of relating. They do emanate a charge when they are together.

In the beginning we compared him to Dad, not bit by bit but in the mere fact of his presence. He knew and he was gracious. He let us be cruel to him and ignore him when we visited our mother and he was there. He never demanded anything. He is still and certain looking, but there is a side to his silence that is the result of repression rather than the hush of wisdom, which means he is great fun to tease.

And he allows Mum her grief, and there is still a pull; I see it on Dad's anniversary and his birthday when we go to the grave. George doesn't go; he accepts that Mum's relationship with Dad has to go on and that their life together isn't finished and that he is still with her.

The drama returned to my mother's life, it was a joy to see it, but in a different way or maybe a way I could accept. She learned to shoot, and that was a turning point in her life. The power of the gun and the potential destruction, it was a comfort to her and it put her madness in perspective. She became an excellent markswoman. She began to compete. She was so herself wherever she went that she stunned people. She would be invited to stalk deer in Scotland or blow away pheasant in England or cull kangaroos in central Australia. It didn't matter where she went, people always commented that they had never met anyone so clearly free to be herself. It was the perfect balance for

her, shooting and fishing and her hunk. She had finally
found a flatter path for a while.

Outside her new house is a poinciana tree, not as big
and grand as the one in the yard of her old house. It's a
miniature, not yet matured, but its branches hang to the
ground. There is a row of them; they stretch all the way
down both sides of the street to the bay at the end of the
road. I sometimes imagine the dead in all of them, stepping across from tree to tree.

About the Author

JUDY PASCOE was born and educated in Australia. She worked for many years as an acrobat before becoming a stand-up comedienne. She has also worked as an actor and scriptwriter.

About the Text

French type designer Jean Lochu, whose training as a designer is rooted in the classical tradition, is said to have designed the Loire typeface "with the Garamond spirit." Lochu's early love of calligraphy and apprenticeship in a small printing shop led to what would become an illustrious career in the typographic arts. In 1968 he met French type designer Albert Hollenstein, who recognized his talent and gave him the opportunity to design his own typefaces at Hollenstein Studios, where, ever since, he has been creating beautiful, original fonts especially suited for elegant text typography.